JENNI WARD

First published in 2020
by Miraworth Books
ABN 44 964 848 123

MIRAWORTH BOOKS
PO Box 3523, Mount Gambier, SA 5290, Australia

Cover design by Maria Spada Designs
Jenni Ward dragon logo by Ross Zapata
Jenni Ward sorcerer logo by Ayhen Aikawa of A/O Artworks
Stock: Book (Linework Stock) / Swirl (Pattern Magic)

A catalogue record for this
work is available from the
National Library of Australia

For my children.

*Never stop believing
in yourself.
Dreams are as important
as goals are.*

CHAPTER ONE

After lighting the fire, Mary stretched her white hands out towards the small flickering flames that began to dance inside the blackened, stone fireplace. Despite its long sleeves and ankle-length hem, her thin, brown, cotton dress offered little protection from the cold. Her home, the book building, had high ceilings and thick stone walls that made it almost impossible to thoroughly heat the space.

A well-worn tapestry chair sat near the fireplace next to a small walnut side table with legs carved into the shapes of dragons soaring up into the sky. Sitting down, Mary picked up the book on the table and ran her finger along the spine. As a child, Mary had hated dragons, maybe even more than anyone else in the village, since she had lost her entire family the night the books were to be burned. Her opinion had changed with the discovery of the book she now held in her hands, the book that had been tightly wedged into the corner at the far end of a very tall shelf, titled: *Dragons*.

When Mary had first found the book and tugged it from its home, Yansa had warned her, "There are some books best left unread. A little knowledge can be uplifting and refreshing but too much can be the bearer of many consequences." Mary had listened–that time–and replaced the book, conceding that Yansa's knowledge far exceeded her own, and she feared misreading, or misinterpreting, important information.

She had ignored the book as best she could, but the book seemed to call her to it, especially after Yansa passed away. Finally, she dismissed the book-keeper's advice and began reading it. It had been difficult; the book was over three hundred years old. The pages were stuck together along the edge, the ink smeared from the moisture that had seeped in from the exposed edges.

Dragons, Mary learned early on, were not easy to identify. The dragon blood didn't run in families but appeared to be a random phenomenon, unlike sorcerers who inherited their powers from parents. On the pages of the book though she found a series of calculations that could be made about a village, such as the size, number of people, and the crops that nourished them all, that could predict a dragon's arrival in a village. By following the formula, Mary had her lucky number: fifteen. To save and be bound to a dragon would be her way out of the village and finally give her the good luck she craved.

Voices outside stirred her attention, and Mary allowed a smile to play on her lips; her new life was about to begin. In silence, she closed her eyes, thanking whatever higher powers existed in the world. Standing up, Mary smoothed the creases of her dress, checked her snood still tamed her hair so it looked passable, and headed to the passage room to get her shawl.

Walking outside, the cool evening air lingered, and Mary pulled the shawl tight around her shoulders. The villagers' torches lit the scene with flickering indecision. Near the village centre, Mary saw that a large crowd had already gathered around Prater.

Prater's tall stature and solid build made him an imposing figure as he sat astride the cream-coloured mare, flicking the excess of the well-used rope back and forth over his hand. His face, framed with short black hair, intensified the shadowy colouring of his eyes as they watched the crowd. His light brown skin, the only trait he had inherited from his mother, set him apart from the villagers. The horse's right hoof pawed at the ground while her head jerked up and down as the crowd pressed in.

Mary moved closer to get a better look at the man at the other end of the rope, the man who would change her life. Her soft leather-soled shoes moved over the dirt until she stood amongst the other villagers. All around her whispered comments were shared and agreed to with a nod of the head.

"This is the creature responsible for our bad luck. The failing crops. The dead cattle. He will pay and we will all be better off," Prater's voice cut through the whispering, and the villagers became silent.

"It's not..." the faint whisper of a hoarse voice started but was cut short by a fierce tug on the rope.

From her new vantage point, Mary could see him lying on his stomach. His clothing was in a deplorable state of tatters with one sleeve missing from his shirt and a tear up to his knee on the right leg of his pants. His face was badly swollen and covered in a splatter of blood mixed with the dirt. In the firelight, thick gold cuffs glistened on his wrists, in stark comparison to the grime that coated his clothes and skin. Mary's cherished book had said nothing of gold, but other books indicated it as being the one thing that could bind a dragon in its human form.

Prater continued his speech about how the dragon would hang at sunrise, but Mary was no longer listening. Her attention was fully on the dragon and she wished for him to look up at her, to see a friendly face, but he did not. To him she was just another person in the crowd, another person calling out for blood and death.

As Prater dismounted, two of his men hurried forward and took the rope knowing the routine well. Together, the men dragged the passive prisoner to the cells. Villagers dispersed, and Mary returned home. Her one chance to set things in motion neared, and she wasn't going to let it pass or leave anything to chance.

Upstairs, Mary collected bread and water from the food cupboard in her bedchamber. When Yansa had taken her in, the hidden room and the tunnels that led away from it had been hers to use and explore, but after he died, she had moved into the bedchamber. At first, she had found the larger space odd but over time became accustomed to it.

With the food in a basket, she checked her appearance in the reflection board that hung on the wall opposite the little window above her bed. Mary observed her dress had a smear of dirt near the collar and that wouldn't do; she changed into a clean dress identical to the one she had removed. Finally, Mary felt that she looked presentable enough for this meeting, and she headed for the detention building.

Smaller than her home, the detention building had only two rooms: the entrance where Prater's desk and chair sat, and the cell where Prater's victims were held. Going into that cell meant the person's fate had been sealed–this thought passed through Mary's mind as she approached the slightly ajar wooden door. She deliberated about knocking, but as she heard no chatter inside decided against it–a quiet building indicated that Prater could be elsewhere, leaving a solitary guard on duty–and pushed the door open.

The guard, Delwyn, scrambled up from his seat when Mary entered. Short and a few years her junior, he hardly appeared suitable to be a guard, but he did follow orders well. She gazed past him, eyeing the large golden door; all that stood between her, the dragon, and her new life.

"That's far enough, Mary," Delwyn's voice sounded commanding but his boyish looks made less than the desired impression.

"I've brought food and water," Mary replied gently with a soft smile on her face.

"He'll be dead at sunrise so why should we bother feeding him?"

Mary flinched at Prater's voice. Turning to face him, she hurriedly brainstormed suitable reasons to justify bringing the food and water. Prater sat casually leaning back into his chair with his feet on the table, watching Mary with curiosity.

At length, she replied, "True, Master Prater, but if he is fed then he can hold nothing against you or our village."

Mary could see Prater thinking over the idea as she managed a half-smile. She found keeping her emotions in check more difficult than she anticipated and fidgeted with the handle of the basket. Even as she stood there, his eyes never left her.

"You've never bothered to bring food and water before Mary – why this time?"

Good question, Mary thought and broke her eye contact with him. Whatever reason she provided, it would need to be good.

"Delwyn," Prater nodded his head towards the door, and Delwyn dutifully left, closing the door behind him. "Tell me, Mary, why this time?"

"I...I..." Mary wanted to kick herself for stammering. It made her sound like she was lying, which she was, but that wasn't the point. "I read something...in a book...about this particular dragon..."

Prater's feet abandoned the table and met the floor with a thud that caused Mary's eyes to jump back to his face. Mary's own feet were anxious to tap, shuffle – to do anything other than remain in one place.

"What about this dragon, Mary?" Prater leaned forward, his hands folded in front of his body as his elbows rested on the empty desk. The light of the candle cast shadows across his face, making his eyes sink back and his cheeks look hollow like the dead.

"He...he...he is different, Master." Mary looked at the basket on her arm. "He will bring bad luck if we do not treat him well before...before..."

"...before he swings from the hanging tree?" he finished for her.

Prater looked away from Mary, and she sighed with relief at the freedom from his gaze. His fingers moved in rhythmic order as she waited for his considered response.

"So, this dragon is more powerful...more valuable even...than the ones who I've dealt with before?"

"Yes." Mary paused for a moment, memories of *that* night flooding her mind before she added, "Yes, he will do more harm than what they did on the night of the burning."

Prater's eyebrows rose before returning to their former position. "More harm? And by feeding him this village will avoid retaliation?"

"The book did not say, Master. It just said that the dragon should be treated well before...before leaving this life."

Mary didn't think what she had said was overly convincing – not that she was known to be a liar or even a gossip in the village, but still she wasn't sure that Prater would believe her. She consoled herself with the thought that he couldn't read so at least he wouldn't be able to refute what she said.

"I don't wish to bring such harm on this village," Prater stated, and Mary looked up in hope. "It wouldn't be fair, and whether you are correct or not about this...this dragon...I need to maintain credibility in this village...in case you are right."

In her mind, Mary sighed once more in relief, but in body, she nodded her agreement with Prater.

"Delwyn! Delwyn get in here."

Delwyn entered the building and returned to where he had stood before. He regarded Prater, waiting to receive any order the Master might demand.

"Mary has a point about feeding this dragon; I don't want him holding anything against the village. Let her in. Have this, Mary." Prater handed her the fancy silver candleholder from his desk, complete with lit candle.

"Shall I be totally safe?" her voice wavered. Mary felt determined to maintain the charade, though her nerves were taking care of the need to pretend to be scared. She glanced down at the basket and tried to keep her fingers still on the handle as she turned towards the door.

"He is bound in gold, dear Mary. He will do you no harm," the words rolled off Prater's tongue in a way that made the hair on Mary's neck stand at attention but she felt some relief now her back faced him.

Delwyn unlocked and opened the gold door to the cell, smiling at Mary as she entered. The cell door closed behind her before her eyes had a chance to adjust. Inside, everything looked black, but then the flickering of the candle's light made shapes emerge from the darkness.

There he sat with his back against the far wall. His wrists and ankles were shackled in gold and his eyes were closed. As Mary stepped closer, she wondered if she wasn't already too late, but the glowing light caught his attention. He looked Mary's way, his eyes sharp and piercing –just like a dragon's should be.

He watched her as she placed the basket down and felt along the wall where it met the floor. Her fingers scraped against the bricks until she found in the corner what the detention blueprints had concealed. She pressed her finger down and, once she'd heard the soft click, covered the corner as best she could with the loose dirt that had blown into the cell at some point.

"I've brought you food and water."

Unable to move from his position due to the restraints, the dragon leaned away from Mary as she knelt down beside him. She placed the candleholder on the stone floor and the basket beside it and busied herself breaking the bread into smaller pieces.

With the bread held in her fingers, she moved closer to the dragon, but he endeavoured to move away again. Even her smile appeared to do nothing to calm him or build any rapport. The thought entered her mind that perhaps, given the circumstance, she appeared scary to him.

"It won't kill you to eat. Look, I'll prove it." Mary ate a piece of bread, making a show out of chewing and swallowing. "See?"

She reoffered him the bread; he didn't turn away. She placed it in his mouth, and he continued to watch her as he chewed it. While he ate, she considered the words she might use; she had practised in her room, but nothing seemed quite right now in the moment.

As she sat down beside him, he continued to eat; when she offered him water from her flask he accepted without hesitation. She noticed he didn't shy away from her being so close, and so, with the candle back in her hand, leaned in closer. "Do you want to get out of here?"

"Of course I do," he replied hoarsely.

"Then we must come to an agreement first," she replied and gave him another piece of bread.

As he chewed the bread, his eyebrows knitted together. "I have money," he offered, but Mary shook her head.

"I don't want money." Mary glanced down at her hands and played with the piece of bread she held before eating it herself.

"Then what?"

"Water?" Mary offered, but he shook his head in refusal, so she continued. "I'm almost seventeen and I am not bound, and since..." she grabbed the gold cuff around his left hand before touching his hand and turning it so that the palm faced the wall, "...you don't have a binding mark, you too are not bound. I do not want to stay in this village forever; it holds too many bad memories. I will help you escape, but only if you agree to be bound to me."

"But I'm already promised to be bound."

"Then you will need to make a decision – die for love or be rescued and live."

Mary moved away to give him space so that he could consider the proposition. Her offer sounded callous even to her own ears, but she had practised those words many times in the safety of her bedchamber in order to sound convincing.

She looked him over as the candle glowed in the otherwise depressing cell. Mary felt his age would be older than her, maybe Prater's age, as she studied the dragon's features. He had a strong build and guessed he would stand taller than her. His brown hair fell across his eyes as he contemplated his future. His pale white skin appeared between dirt, blood and bruises. Mary allowed herself a slight smile; he would indeed make a good husband...which reminded Mary...

"Oh, and don't think I'll rescue you and then you can just take off. If you do, I'll personally put the rope around your neck," and she meant her words, though Mary hated violence as a rule. People had always dismissed her feelings as if they didn't exist. Mary didn't want him to think he could treat her the same way.

The dragon started shaking his head from side to side. "No, I won't agree."

She felt something inside her chest sink and melt away but replaced it with a feeling of annoyance and then anger.

"Fine." Standing up, she bent down to pick up the candleholder from the floor.

A rattle of a chain. "Wait."

Mary watched as he closed his eyes. "We have an agreement?"

"Yes." One small word spoken in defeat; she smiled and left the candle.

"There's a section of the wall that moves. It's connected to the building where I live through a secret passage. I'll come for you later." Mary paused. "First though, we need to make sure that they won't do their checks on you."

"And how will you manage that?" The dragon's tone was both sarcastic and bitter; she knew it would take time for him to develop feelings for her, but she had waited so long–a bit longer wouldn't hurt.

"You'll see," Mary whispered back.

Picking up the basket and candleholder, she knocked twice on the door and waited. Inhaling a deep breath, she suppressed a smile of triumph.

"Ungrateful creature! How dare you say that!" Mary said it loudly enough to be heard as the door was opening. "It will be a pleasure to see you hang." She exited the cell and said directly to Delwyn, "The things he said, and he refused the food! So much for treating him well!"

It seemed wrong to Mary to use her knowledge of the locals to her advantage in such a way, but she saw the eager expression on Delwyn's face as he turned to Prater for permission. She swallowed hard as Prater gave him a cursory nod. Delwyn needed no further encouragement.

"I'll teach him a lesson, Mary."

Mary saw the smile that crossed Delwyn's face as he walked by her towards the cell, crackling his knuckles. Her eyes lingered on the closed door for a moment before she turned and bid Prater farewell and quickly exited the building. She felt guilty knowing that Delwyn would teach the dragon a lesson in the coming hours but took solace in the necessity of it. At least once Delwyn had exacted the punishment, the dragon would be left alone, and because he would be alone, she hoped that her plan would be executed flawlessly.

Pausing for a moment, Mary closed her eyes and breathed in the cool air. She smiled knowing that the book building stood only a few steps away. With eyes open again, she adjusted the basket on her arm. A hand on that same arm made Mary jump, and she turned to see that Prater had followed her.

"I appreciate you looking out for the village, and me as well," Prater began as he looked down at Mary.

"This village has been through enough already."

"You know, if you're free tomorrow, I heard there's a patch of wildflowers near the old bridge, we could go for a walk after we've dealt with the dragon if you want."

"Perhaps we could. Goodnight, Master Prater."

CHAPTER TWO

Time passed slowly as Mary waited for the sun to go down and then waited even longer for the chatter of the people outside to fade to silence. Finally, when all signs of people had disappeared outside, she lit the candle and descended the half dozen steps from the passage room to one that sat to the left, known as the narrow book room. In that room, the oldest of the books were stored away from the sunlight to preserve their contents longer.

As she walked to a particular bookcase in the middle of the longest wall that ran parallel with the passage room's walls, she found it difficult to contain the elation and excitement she felt. Reaching up to the shelf just above her head, she pulled on the spine of the book *Tiani's Local Customs and Celebrations* to free it from its place.

Once the book was in her hand, she reached for the back of the bookcase and pushed down on a small lever. For a moment nothing happened, and Mary replaced the book as if it had never been removed. Then, slowly and silently, a section of the bookcase moved backwards, and then to the right-hand side, revealing the secret tunnel.

Stepping into the tunnel, Mary turned and pressed down on another lever, this one larger and not concealed by the entrance way. She did not bother to watch the bookcase close and instead focused on the sight before her.

Normally, she would face the endless darkness of the tunnel ahead, but she had prepared it in advance by collecting the sap from the trees behind the book building. The sap allowed for the torches to burn longer when the sticks were soaked in it overnight. Even though they'd been alight since morning, they continued cast light in the tunnel for the first part of the journey.

Passing them by, she tapped the pocket of her apron to assure herself that she hadn't forgotten the extra candles and matches that she would need. Above ground, the detention building might be a short walk away, but it wasn't the case in the tunnels.

When the tunnel had been built, the book-keeper had been concerned about it collapsing or the earth sagging from travel over it by the villagers, and decided that a direct path would be noticeable if something went wrong. The plans were then made to ensure that the tunnel, or series of tunnels as it became, weaved and curved some distance to the outskirts of Tiani, both where the sun rose and where it set.

Walking along the dirt floor of the tunnel, Mary allowed her fingers to trail lightly across the smoothness of the stone walls. She waited to feel the texture of the stone change as it would indicate to her that she would be close to the cell's wall. Finally, she felt that change; it was rougher, and the stones were not so neatly joined.

Mary held her hand over her chest to encourage her heart to become steadied in pace. With an exhale of breath, she drew closer to the wall, pressed her ear up against the stone doorway, and listened. A few moans of pain broke the silence, and Mary bit her lip, knowing that she wouldn't be the dragon's favourite person straight away.

Pressing hard on one particular brick in the wall, a soft click sounded before a section began to move silently to the side. In the place of the bricks, a hole big enough for any adult to climb through appeared.

Before she entered, Mary reached out and with effort placed the candleholder on the floor in the room. She moved her head carefully through the hole and her body followed swiftly until she stood inside the cell.

She fumbled in her pocket amongst the spare candles for the key, a master key to unlock the chains. She had obtained it some months prior when Prater had fallen drunk from his horse and passed out near the entrance of the book building. Books had certainly come in handy to learn how to make a mould. She had identified a local tree that, when cut, oozed thick sticky amber-coloured sap, though she had to work quickly to mould the sap around the key and remove it before it became entombed. The books had also versed her on how to then melt down one of the two spoons she owned to create the key.

"How could you do that?" the dragon hissed before sucking his breath in quickly. His hands clutched at his side where the mark of a boot stained the remains of the shirt.

Mary unlocked his right wrist as she knelt next to him. "You want to stay here?"

He shook his head as the lock opened, freeing one wrist, then the other, before his ankles were freed as well.

Mary helped him stand, and he staggered to the opening in the wall. The dragon gingerly lifted his leg up and hoisted himself into the tunnel– almost toppling in head first – and Mary followed silently.

With the cell behind them, they started the walk back to the book building. It took longer than she had anticipated due to the injuries he had sustained at the hands of both Prater and Delwyn. There were times that Mary struggled to help him walk as his arm weighed heavily across her shoulders. Finally, she led him to a room to the side of the entrance through the bookcase. She felt that it would be better and safer if he rested for a few days first. Plus, if Prater ordered a building search, then the dragon would not be found, as she was the only person alive who knew of the room's existence.

As the dragon sat on the bed, Mary took a look at his wrists. They were red and abraded but some bruising had also begun to form from the pressure of the cuffs. Her forehead creased at the sight, concerned that the gold had started to affect him so soon. No written records existed of the real effect gold had on a dragon; the information in the books fell closer to being conjecture and legend, the kind of story Mary's own mother had told her as a child.

Mary turned away from the dragon to light the fire that must have burned out during the rescue. Once the flames were blazing, Mary picked up the black metal pot she had filled with water the previous day, removed the covering cloth, and hooked it above the heat.

A silence hung over the room as Mary waited for the water to begin to boil. She tried to keep her attention on the fire to avoid the glare of the dragon behind her. Still, even as her fingers impatiently tapped against her apron, she felt uncomfortable at the situation she had created.

As the water began to dance on the surface, Mary used the covering cloth to remove the pot and set it down on the stone floor. She turned and picked up a thicker cloth from the small wooden table beside the bed, along with a wooden bowl that sat beside it. Back at the pot, Mary poured the water into the bowl, careful not to spill any. Steam rose from the bowl but subsided a little when she added a couple of cups of cold water from the original barrel. Mary hesitantly turned and walked the water over to the dragon, placing the bowl down on the table it had come from.

"Leave me alone." He pushed Mary away and lay down so that he faced the stone wall.

"Don't be such a baby." She dunked the thicker cloth into the bowl and then twisted it to remove some of the water. While he didn't say anything, she noticed how his head turned at the sound.

She rolled him over and started to wash his left hand and wrist, revealing the pale white skin of the northern region of the kingdom. The dragon had his head turned to the right, concentrating on the wall. Mary remembered a time when she too had found that wall fascinating.

"The wound is deep, but it will heal in time." She paused, "I'm Mary."

As the dragon turned his head to look at her, Mary began washing his other arm. She glanced up to see that his expression remained stern and unfriendly.

"I can wash myself." He tried grabbing the cloth, but Mary pulled it out of reach.

"Sure, just like you can walk without help." She smiled and the dragon let out a low growl.

Rinsing the cloth, Mary reached out to wash his neck, but his hand caught her wrist and his grip tightened. The show of strength both surprised and puzzled her; if the legends were true, a dragon's body couldn't recover so quickly. She pushed the thought away, reminding herself that she'd never read anything in a book to confirm the legend, but made a mental note to ask later on, when he recovered.

"I said I can do it."

Mary handed him the cloth and he let go.

"Fine. There's a change of clothes over there." Getting up, she began walking towards the door before realising he hadn't even thanked her. Her pride prickled. "You really are ungrateful."

Outside of the room, Mary reached for the lever and left him alone. Upstairs in the main book room, Mary could see the lightened sky outside as the night began to fade away. Despite the night being long, she didn't feel as sleepy as she had anticipated.

In her bedchamber, she exchanged her brown dress for a black one before descending the staircase in no great hurry. Mary grabbed her shawl that hung from a hook beside the door and wrapped it around her shoulders.

The villagers had gathered by the hanging tree. The sun would rise at any moment, and the absence of Prater could be heard in the chatter. Mary hid the smile she wanted to show and looked around at the other villagers, mimicking their confused looks.

A hushed silence came over the crowd as Prater emerged from his own home. Mary had never entered Prater's home but had heard rumours of it containing no less than four bedchambers, far more than any others in the village. She had overheard these details from the leaders who often walked past the book building after dark to smoke their pipes. Mary supposed that behind the imposing oak door that had weathered with age, rooms of pure wonderment must be concealed. Yet her curiosity had never been piqued enough to tempt her inside.

Prater stood beneath the tree, and Mary noticed that for the moment he seemed unphased and at ease. Delwyn hurried from the cells with a look of surprise, bewilderment and fear. Upon seeing Delwyn, Prater's demeanour abruptly changed.

"He's gone, the dragon has escaped!" Delwyn exclaimed, his voice pitching higher than usual, as he came up close to Prater.

A murmur from those villagers nearest to Prater went up before a silence descended, an eerie silence that Mary had heard only once before. The thought of that event sent a shiver down Mary's back and she pulled the shawl tighter.

Mary observed with the group as Prater stooped over awkwardly to hear Delwyn. He clenched his fists and set his jaw.

"That's impossible!" Prater hissed back before casting a look at the crowd and taking a breath.

Delwyn looked at the ground as he tried to whisper, "He's not in there; the cell is empty. What should we do?"

"Get my horse and gather the men," Prater ordered, and Delwyn immediately moved to complete the task.

Prater turned to the gathered crowd. The collective voices made intended whispers become audible as the conversation the men had exchanged filtered through the crowd. With his hand raised, Prater said, "A minor setback. He will be found and hung. Go ahead and start your daily duties."

As the other villagers moved back towards their homes, and the men gathered outside the detention building, Mary slipped back into the book building very pleased that her plan remained on course.

Preparing some food, Mary felt that the dragon should have had enough time to calm down. After all, according to what she had read, dragons were supposed to be unable to break promises. However, Mary still questioned what she read in books, which was why she had warned him in the cell of breaking it – just in case.

Mary found him where she left him, on the bed. She noted with pleasure that he had taken the time to clean himself and now wore the clothes she had left for him. He glanced her way when she entered, but his eyes wandered quickly away from her and to the food on the plate she carried.

Mary placed the plate down on the table next to the bed. Eagerly, he reached out for the food and started to push it into his mouth in a most undignified manner as Mary turned for the door.

"You've eaten already?"

Mary paused and turned to face him. "You need it more than me."

He sat back, leaving the remainder of the food uneaten.

"Eat," he said, indicating the plate with his hand. It was the first sign of civility Mary had received from him.

"You'll need your strength. I cannot increase the food ration they give me. I'll be fine; go ahead and eat."

"Is that an order?" He had a playful look in his eye that made Mary relax somewhat in his company.

"Yes, it is."

"What if I don't?"

"Then we will both go hungry." A simple and clear fact that needed no further explanation, but as Mary waited for his response, she saw his eyes look over her. She pursed her lips, hoping to convey her determination.

"I could leave at any time."

"Yes, you could, but then I would be forced to keep my promise to you." As Mary spoke the words, there was no hint of playfulness in her tone or facial expression. She didn't like to threaten but she wanted the good luck; she felt she deserved the good luck after what had happened to her family. "I need to go."

Away from the dragon, she slid down the wall and pulled her knees up. Memories of that night flooded her mind and played as if it had happened only yesterday. It had been a dark, starless night; most nights the villagers were in bed when the sunset, as most rose early to start work.

That night though, people from neighbouring villages had travelled to witness the burning. Prater, the new village leader and no more than a teenager, had ordered the men of the village to build a fire larger than had ever been needed. His reason had been simple: all the books were to be burned.

Yansa, the elderly book-keeper with the tanned earth-brown face, weather-beaten and wrinkled, had tried to stop him, but had been overpowered by men a third of his age, men who didn't suffer the complaints that age bought with it. Those men held him to the side as the events unfolded. Yansa told Mary years later, that at that time he had been the sole person who could read in the village despite years of trying to convince others of the importance of books.

People gathered around the fire, all eyes on Prater. He smiled as he looked around, waiting to enact his first command as master of Tiani. Prater had been appointed to the position after the sudden death of his father, making him the youngest leader in the area.

The crowd hushed as Prater raised his arm in readiness for his speech, but Yansa had seen his chance to speak.

"You mustn't burn the books," the old man cried out. "The dragons...the dragons will be angry. You cannot use their power to destroy something they work to preserve. They will..." A vicious blow delivered by one of Prater's men knocked the breath from Yansa's mouth.

Bent over in pain wheezing, his arms held tightly by the men, Yansa's eyes filled with a look of sadness, that as a six-year-old, she'd been unable to understand. Mary's hand clung tightly to the long skirt of her mother, who had patted her head; the habit had always soothed her but not that night. She watched with all the others, her brown eyes open wide, as the flames licked at the night air in anticipation.

"We will burn these useless books and make the book building a place for us all!" Prater picked up the first book, a conceited smile on his face.

Yansa closed his eyes and raised his hands to cover his face. Mary remembered doing the same thinking it a game.

The book never touched the fire. It didn't even get close enough to be singed.

Mary opened her eyes to find Prater turning in a bewildered circle in the midst of dozens of villagers lying on the ground. The book in his hand wavered in the air until it fell to the ground beside his feet. His hand covered his mouth as the survivors began to curse and cry.

Mary reached for her mother's skirt but grasped only air. Looking down, she found that her mother had fallen, along with her father and older sister. She knelt beside her mother and shook her shoulders.

"Mama, wake up. Mama, Mama!" She had shaken her mother as hard as she could, but when her mother would not even blink, she crawled towards her father who lay nearby. "Papa, Papa, you need to get up. Papa, open your eyes." She reached for her sister next. "Jessie? Jessie, I'm gonna eat that cake Mama left on the table for you. I swear I will if you don't open your eyes!"

Hands encircled her and tried to lift her away from her sister.

"No! Let me go!" Mary kicked and scratched until the hands released her and she crawled back towards her family, lying down beside her mother, clutching her warm hand and tugging on it every now and then. "Why won't they open their eyes? How come they won't wake up?"

Mary looked up at the person who had tried to hold her before and saw the boy her mother had considered too arrogant to be a leader. He trembled and reached out his hand, which Mary swatted away.

"This is your fault. They won't wake up because of you!"

He opened his mouth, but another man strode past Prater and turned so his back obscured her line of sight. "I think you've done enough for tonight. Let the girl grieve."

Mary wiped her eyes at the rawness of the memory. She shivered as she remembered how she had clasped her mother's hand until the warmth left her. Prying her hand away had taken some effort on Yansa's part. She sniffed and used her sleeve to wipe her face of the tears.

CHAPTER
THREE

Prater had been in a foul temper since the dragon had escaped several weeks before, and Mary had tried to avoid him as much as possible. Still, she hadn't been surprised to be stirred away from the book she sat reading by a knock at the door.

"Master."

"It's such a nice afternoon; I thought we might take a walk, look at those wildflowers."

Mary glanced back towards where she had left her book, knowing she would much rather have continued with it. Instead, she nodded and took Prater's offered arm. They walked down the street and turned onto a little dirt trail.

She'd walked to the old river bridge many times over the years. The river had dried up a long time ago, but a variety of wildflowers painted the shores where it had once run.

"How goes the search?" Mary ventured. She grabbed a dragon-rose from a bush beside the trail as they ambled past, admiring the vibrant blue colouring.

"Not well, I should probably give up searching. My father used to say that if you couldn't find what you'd lost within a day, then you weren't meant to have it."

Her fingers felt the softness of the rose petals, giving her something to focus on. "Perhaps it is a sign that strangers should be welcomed once again."

"I trusted the word of a stranger once, with disastrous consequences. No, I can't allow that mistake again." The comment piqued Mary's curiosity and she wondered at who the stranger could have been. Prater had justified his insistence on ensuring strangers stayed away from Tiani by claiming they were dragons, and people still believed that dragons ate people.

"The village will die without more people though. Each year it gets older, and there's so few of us that are younger." Only a handful of children had survived the burning, and they were all now approaching adulthood or already there. A few had left for the larger cities, others had family elsewhere; most just hadn't wanted to stay and be reminded daily of their loss.

"I know, Mary, that's been on my mind too of late."

The bridge came into view and Mary moved off and crouched to pick some of the flowers, choosing the white sprays of delicate buds, the blue forget-me-nots, and yellow-orange marigolds. She reached out and tugged a couple of the large leaves from the base of the sprays free, using them to wrap it all into a bouquet. Standing she looked over to see Prater smiling in her direction.

"That's very beautiful."

Mary shrugged. She'd read a few books on how to arrange flowers but her own attempts never looked as refined as she liked. Still, they would brighten up a corner with their splash of colour, bringing some life with them.

"They won't be here much longer."

Mary knew Prater as right about that. Today the sky had remained clear, but the cooler winds had been slowly moving the warmth of the sun away towards the south of the kingdom.

"Perhaps you could make me one, too. I have a vase on my mantel that always seems to be empty."

Nodding, Mary busied herself picking flowers to make a second one, though she replaced the blue forget-me-nots with red bellflowers. Once bundled in leaves, she offered the posy to him. His fingers brushed against the back of her hand, and she bit her lip for a moment.

"You know, we're not so unalike, are we Mary?"

"I'm not sure."

Prater laughed and offered his arm again as they started back towards the village. "I guess, what I meant is that we get along alright. I'm always so busy protecting Tiani, I never venture too far away from here. I mean, we both live in the village, and our ages are not so different, only nine years. Not that much really."

Mary's finger twitched, concealed beneath the leaf. She had no intentions of remaining in the village and being bound to Prater. When she had first gone to look for books in the nearby villages several months before, she had seen how the people smiled more than in Tiani.

"I don't want to stay always in Tiani, Master. There is so much I would like to see before I make a home with someone." Part of her felt she should remain for the sake of the books, but her heart told her that she needed to leave to find her own place in the kingdom – she just needed a little good luck to make it happen.

Prater sighed but said nothing more. Ahead, Mary felt pleased to see the street into Tiani emerging into view. The sun had already disappeared, leaving the sky resembling the wildflower patch.

"Maybe we could walk again tomorrow?"

"Maybe." Mary shifted her feet on the step and reached to turn the door handle.

"Mary?"

She hadn't completely turned back to him when she felt a light kiss on her cheek. Her eyes darted to his face as he smiled and stepped away.

"Until tomorrow then, Mary." He walked away without waiting for a reply, and Mary slipped inside, sliding the bolt to lock the door.

In the privacy of her room, she looked into the reflection board and touched her cheek. The lingering touch brought thoughts of being bound to him to the forefront of her mind. Mary held him responsible for what happened to her family and she knew that would always cause her blood to run cold.

Prater's voice floated through her window, and she sat on the bed looking down towards the detention building. With her room in darkness, she knew the moonlight might betray her, but she watched on despite it.

She couldn't hear the words but saw Prater point Delwyn towards the north end of the village. Both men nodded, and Mary knew her chances to escape were diminishing if Prater's focus on finding the missing dragon wavered and he kept his men close to the village's boundary. Turning away from the window she glanced around the familiar room making her decision.

The dragon looked up with eyebrows raised as Mary hurried into the room. She brushed it aside and took in his improved appearance – despite still being discoloured, the swelling around the dragon's eye had subsided, and the cuts had healed over.

"We go tonight."

"Where to?" he questioned, seeming a little uneasy.

"To a town nearby: Haversy."

"So, by this time tomorrow I'll be a bound man?"

Mary looked over at him; his unhappiness with what he had promised came through clear, but she felt happy nevertheless. "Yes."

They left through yet another tunnel underneath the book building, this one exiting outside of the village boundary. A series of large rocks concealed the opening hidden deep in the forest and away from any roads where they might be seen. Mary and the dragon walked into the town of Haversy in silence, and she couldn't shake the feeling that the approaching binding equalled a kind of death for him. A deal had been struck, and dragons had to keep their word like everyone else.

At the village gathering building, Mary found the binding man. It was a simple ceremony with his wife and son as witnesses to the event. When they left the gathering building, Mary and the dragon had identical black binding marks with their binding record number entwined in the pattern on their left hands — the magic of the dragons.

No words were spoken as they located a suitable inn where Mary bartered for a room, handing over an engraved silver hand reflection board that had once belonged to her mother. At the binding service, the dragon had given the name Michael. She wasn't convinced he had been truthful but accepted it all the same. He gave no other names; most people, like Mary, only had the one. Titles only belonged to the very rich or powerful who mostly lived in the great cities. Titles did not matter though, as the dragons bound the souls of the two together – names were completely irrelevant.

In the room, the dragon still hadn't said anything to Mary, and she felt a pang of disappointment. She had on her hand what she had wanted, and now that they were bound, she would be blest. She waited for him to reveal himself as a dragon. Instead though, he stood leaning against the wall, staring at his hand.

Her eyes travelled around the room, and she walked around the straw bed to be nearer the window and as far away from Michael as she could get.

"You hate me." Mary turned to look out the window. In the distance, black rain clouds were rolling in from the direction of the Great Forest, enveloping everything in their path into darkness.

"I'm bound to you," he replied from the other side of the room. "I never said I'd love you or do anything else."

Looking away from the window, Mary watched as Michael slumped down onto the wooden floor, still leaning against the wall.

"You take the bed," he said.

Mary continued to stare out of the window. "No, you take the bed. I'm not tired."

"We've been travelling all day; if I'm tired then you certainly must be too."

Tears welled behind Mary's eyes, but she wasn't going to let them fall. *Surely if he's a dragon he would say so? Shouldn't I know about the good luck? What if I my calculations were wrong?* She didn't want to consider that thought.

She remembered back to the day she had dislodged the old book from the shelf. The book with the two entwined dragons on the cover and the simple title of: *Dragons*. Water-stained and covered in mould, she had to clean the book up first to be near it without coughing. Her curiosity had outweighed her mentor's warning, and night after night she had poured over the ancient pages until she reached a section about luck.

That one chapter on luck she read over and over. It contained the formula for predicting future events based on the location, year, and even the day. The formula though had been incomplete. Ink streaked down one side of the page, making the last couple of words on each line a mystery, but she had read it enough to know that there had been just one important number on the page that she couldn't read well. Mary had stared at that one blur longer than the reading had taken until, confident she had it correct, she calculated the next dragon that would come Tiani's way. She had thought the margin of error so small it worth the risk, but fifteen had been wrong. It should have been sixteen.

"You're not a dragon, are you?" her words were no more than a disappointed whisper.

"A dragon? Of course not. I tried to tell them I was innocent, that I wasn't a dragon...is that the only reason you rescued me?" The harshness of his tone felt like an accusation, and Mary bit her lip.

"Never mind."

Michael shook his head, and she heard the growl that escaped from his lips. "Look, Mary, take the bed."

"Don't bother with kindness now. As you said, you've done all you agreed to do."

Mary continued to stare at the window, aware of his reflection looking back at her. He opened his mouth as if to say something, then changed his mind. He moved over to the straw bed and lay down.

She knew when he started to sleep from the change in his breathing. Mary switched from watching his reflection to her own. A tear fell from her eye and rolled down the side of her face, the only one she let escape.

When morning arrived and she heard Michael stirring, Mary remained at the window, observing the rooves of the buildings set against a clear sky. With the light, she could see the tips of the trees that filled the Great Forest in the distance and knew beyond that, home waited.

"Did you sleep at all?" he asked, and Mary didn't reply. "What will you do now?"

Mary looked down to the floor, away from the window. "That's not your concern."

"Actually, it is. I'm your husband now and you are my responsibility."

Finally, Mary turned away from the window to look at him. Yesterday everything had seemed so clear, but now her luck seemed nowhere to be found.

"Go home to your promised," she replied, and then turned back to the window. She just couldn't look at him any longer, look at what might and could have been, that now wouldn't be.

"And how am I to explain this?" he countered, pointing at the binding mark on his hand. "First you rescue me, make me be bound to you, and now you want me to leave?"

"It's what you wanted, to leave." Mary turned to him, wanting to say it to his face. "Tell them I died. Tell them it was a stupid girl's dying wish you granted."

"But what…"

"I'm old enough to take care of myself, whoever, whatever, you are."

"They will know you are not dead! You know how these bindings work…how am I…what…"

"I'm sure you can come up with some reason…or maybe you can pay someone to undo it. You have such a high opinion of yourself that I suppose you have the wealth to back it up." The bitter tone surprised Mary, but she felt keenly the disappointment of everything she had done resulting in nothing.

"I won't leave until I know you have work, until I know you are able to take care of yourself properly. I might not be a dragon, but I'm not a monster either."

With a cynical smile, Mary turned to him. "I hardly have any other choice, woman are rarely paid for their work."

"But you worked with the books…"

"I was not paid. The food was guilt, or pity, both maybe, who knows which, for the past."

"What happened?"

"Again, that's none of your business."

He let out a sigh of frustration, a reflection of Mary's own feelings.

"Come with me."

"What, and pretend none of this happened? It's clear you resent me; that wouldn't be a good situation for either of us." Furious, Mary turned back to the safety of the view from the window.

After some time, she heard him open the door and leave. Turning around, Mary sighed at the solitude. *Was it really such a big request that I should be happy? To know what it is like to have someone care for me as much as I do for them?*

Two days later, Mary arrived back where it all started. On her hands she wore gloves to hide the binding mark, a constant reminder of how easily a plan could go wrong, a reminder of how she had made a mistake and how dangerous books could be.

Walking along the main road, Mary wondered if anyone would have noticed her gone. She often travelled between neighbouring villages to collect discarded books and papers but had always returned. As if to answer the question, she observed the food in the box in front of the door. She licked her lips at the sight and heard the growl of her empty stomach.

Inside the book building, Mary lit a candle with a match that she had picked up from the tin box beside it. Walking forward, Mary turned right into the main book room. She looked at the familiar books that reached up high on the walls to the ceiling, stairs going everywhere so that every book was accessible without too much effort. When Mary had been little, she had thought that the book building was pure magic. The thought brought a momentary smile to her face.

The book that had led to the mess she faced came to mind. She considered if maybe she had done the calculations for what she wanted, rather than what they told. *What if it wasn't a dragon but just a man? Had I believed in it so hard because I wanted it to be true? Should I rescue the next man to be caught by Prater, or should I stop making such a fool of myself?*

Why is it that we always have more questions than answers? All my life I have found answers to my questions in the books that surround me every day. Now though they seem so empty of everything I have always thought they held.

Walking back to the passage room, Mary untied her cape as she trudged up the stairs to retire to her bedchamber. Her arms carried the bundles of food that she had collected from the box. She just wanted to go to sleep and wake up a week in the past so she could stop herself from doing what she had.

In Mary's bedchamber, she hung her shawl next to the reflection board. Her eyes were drawn to the girl who stared blankly back at her. She had never considered herself beautiful, maybe a little pretty when the lights were low and soft, but she saw a face staring back at her that appeared to have lost its soul.

Mary placed the food down on the table near her bed and changed her clothes. Her hand picked up a bread roll, but she couldn't bring herself to take a bite. With her hunger dissipated, she opted for crawling into bed and snuggling down as far as she could under the quilt she had made five years before. Closing her eyes, she allowed herself to be transported to another place where life was much simpler, easier, and always had the ending she wanted.

Quinn narrowed his eyes on the map in his hands, frustrated. He'd spent most of the previous night going over it, trying to commit it to memory without luck. Only that morning he'd grumbled about how old the map's details were, and now as he stood in the middle of a road, he growled in annoyance.

He'd purposefully planned his arrival in the Great Forest, knowing the thick trees would conceal his every movement, to prevent any panic arising from villagers who might bear witness. As it turned out, he had appeared on the very road he stood on – in full view of anyone who might have been around.

"Give me a break," he muttered and folded the map, tucking it away inside his coat.

Walking along the road, the trees of the Great Forest were within sight, but he saw that a village loomed on the horizon – that hadn't been on the map either. With each step he took, he reminded himself of his purpose. The same task he'd been trying to complete for years without success. He'd told himself a number of times that he could quit and just do what he wanted, but duty and an oath compelled him to act unselfishly.

As the village came into view, a middle-aged man, bent over in half as he carried a large bale of hay on his back, walked steadily towards him. When the man looked up, Quinn paused and tried to gauge his reaction.

"What brings you out this way, young man?"

Quinn bit his tongue at the wording; he reminded himself that being referred to as young shouldn't grate his nerves. "I'm just looking for a relative who might have come this way."

"You'd do well not to enquire around here. Strangers, you see, aren't welcome in these parts, especially the further you go down this road."

"I'll take your warning under advisement." Quinn nodded to end the greeting and continued past the man.

"Your funeral then!" The words caught Quinn's attention and his pace slowed. He turned to see the man walking away down the road. Usually, he didn't rattle so easily. He knew he shouldn't; if the villagers saw his power, then they'd be the ones running.

At the village, Quinn looked around trying to carefully choose who to approach. A woman sat weaving a basket on the step of a wooden house.

"Have you seen..?" Quinn pointed to the piece of paper he held in his hand, and the woman leaned forward.

"Well that's a mighty fine drawing. You one of those fancy artist types from the city then?"

"It's not my work. I'm trying to find this person."

"Hmm," the woman murmured and turned back to her basket.

"Is it possible that someone could have passed through here without being noticed?"

"Of course, we're not awake at all hours just to watch for people." Her hand pushed the reed through, and she pointed down the road. "Just you be careful around these parts. Strangers aren't much welcomed here."

"You're the second person to say that today."

"Perhaps it's time you listened then. Now be off, I need to get this finished."

Quinn raised his eyebrows. He hadn't encountered such strange behaviour before, and he'd been on the receiving end of some very odd behaviour in his search.

Moving away from the woman, he headed down the dusty road. Houses stood on either side, with many of their occupants watching as he passed by. The adults seemed wary of him, and he looked around hoping to ask a child or two because in his experience, they were less likely to lie. He paused; he saw no children playing beside the houses, or running through the trees a short distance away.

"Well that's a little creepy." He shook off the feeling and left the town but felt compelled to turn and look back before following the curve of the road. Behind him he saw villagers standing in a group, staring in his direction. "Humans are far too complicated."

Still, as a little house appeared on the road ahead, he slowed his pace and then stopped altogether. The words of those in the last village repeated in his mind and he looked off to the side. The Great Forest, according to the map, covered much of the area. He hoped that maybe he could sneak a look at the village without entering it, and the trees would provide a good amount of cover.

As he stepped off the path and into the shade of the forest trees, he thought about the picture in his pocket. He'd been gone from home for nearly two weeks on his search, and he longed to sleep in his own bed, in clean clothes, and get rid of the beard that graced his face.

A branch snagged on his pants, and Quinn had to stop to free it. The nearby brambles scratched at his hands as he finally freed the last stubborn thread. The undergrowth continued to cause Quinn issues, and he breathed with relief when he found a path. It didn't look too much better than the wildness he'd just walked through, but the narrow little piece of dirt trailing around the trees would be better than nothing.

The path took a twist to the left before turning sharply to the right. Quinn looked up trying to see the sun in the sky to get a bearing, but the trees hid it away. He growled in frustration before his foot caught on a rock. His arms stretched out to attempt to break his fall but failed. Rolling over several times, Quinn reached up to touch his head. Trying to stand up, his foot slipped from beneath him and sent him tumbling forward again. His head hit against something hard and darkness blinded him.

Quinn's eyes opened for a moment, and everything looked blurry, so he blinked once, twice. With his eyes squinting, he rolled from his back onto his side. His hand reached up and rubbed at his aching shoulder. He heard a crunching noise and moved his head down so he could see his knees. A pair of black boots appeared, and then its owner prodded him in the chest.

"You down there," Prater's voice boomed above him.

"What?" Quinn's hoarse voice replied, and he attempted to look up towards the owner of the boots.

"Dragon, I presume." The voice failed to wait for Quinn to reply. "Who are you?"

"Just looking for someone, maybe you've seen..."

"You don't belong here."

Quinn felt the boot kick hard into his stomach, and he cringed at the pain that shot through his body. Instinctively, he pulled his knees closer to his waist to try and foil any other kicks that might come.

"Look, I'm not looking for trouble, I'm just..."

"Looking for someone, right?"

Quinn felt uneasy being circled like some kind of prey and wished he'd listened to the villagers who had warned him.

"I don't like strangers around these parts."

"I don't want any trouble; I'll just be on my way then." Quinn reached out his hands and pushed himself up. He breathed in sharply as his shoulder objected to the movement.

"Now, now what's the hurry then?" The man extended his hand, and Quinn finally managed to look up and see a vague impression of the man's face.

"I have been travelling for a while. I would like to get home."

Stubbornly, Quinn got to his own feet and felt relieved to find that while other parts of his body objected, his sore feet appeared okay to walk on. Quinn hadn't managed to stand up straight, but he did get a sense of the height of the man who stood a head taller than he did.

"First, let's do a little test and see if you are a dragon...or not?"

Quinn rolled his eyes, wondering what sort of foolish nonsense the man would attempt. He'd heard of tests that included being tied to a chair and dunked in water, being pushed from a cliff to see if one could fly and eating the hot peppers from the south – to see if one could breathe fire, of course.

"Fine, let's get it over with then."

"Hold out your hands."

Quinn held out his hands, waiting. He saw the gold cuffs in the man's hand and recoiled at the sight. His instinct betrayed his own fear, and when Quinn looked up, he saw the smile that had spread across the man's face.

The man grabbed one hand and locked the cuff in place. Quinn struggled against the man, but the journey and fall had taken their toll. The gold just further complicated his situation. As the coolness of the gold encircled both wrists, his vision became intermittent. Quinn's legs felt weak. When he landed hard on the ground, he heard the laugh, and then felt the pain as blows struck at his body.

CHAPTER
FIVE

For the first couple of days after Mary returned to Tiani, she barely left the book building, though she did nothing within it either. Mary had not touched a book but to put it back on a shelf since she had returned from Haversy, but she knew that she would have to leave the security of the book building eventually.

That day did come when the last of the water in the barrel ran dry. Located near the hanging tree, the well stood a short distance from the book building but across the divide of dirt that separated the buildings in town. Several of the villagers had looked at her gloves as she drew the pail up from the well, but Mary dismissed it by telling them she had an accident with boiling water in a neighbouring village and had scarred her hands. No one asked any more questions.

Mary had lost interest in the books that had once filled so much of her time. No men had been hanged in her time away, which meant he was still to come, number sixteen. She considered trying to ignore the fact that the next of Prater's victims would be a dragon. Sure, she'd have good luck if she rescued him also, but it wouldn't be the lead to the future she'd imagined. Of course, if Mary didn't rescue him and he hung, that would bring her bad luck for knowingly letting him die.

Tapping her fingers on the wooden desk, Mary considered which would be the worse possibility –being cursed for life and not knowing what she had missed out on, or knowing what life could have been like if she weren't so foolish but having good luck. To Mary, the decision felt akin to choosing how she wanted to die; neither something she wanted but inevitable all the same.

As she sat at the desk, fingers tapping, raised voices outside drew her thoughts from the possibility to the reality, and Mary knew that the time had come. Walking to the front door, Mary gazed out upon the scene taking place just metres away. Like some surreal recreation, Prater sat high on his cream steed amongst the gathered people. Mary's eyes followed the rope, gripped tightly in

Prater's left hand, to the gold handcuffs around the wrists of a man.

The man differed substantially from last time. Unlike Michael, he didn't struggle to free himself, his voice wasn't protesting his innocence. From a distance, he even looked dead. His clothes were tattered and torn, particularly around the hems, and a layer of brown earth mixed with blood, both dried and fresh, covered the man's dishevelled clothing. At no point did he move as Mary watched through the window in the book building's door. The only movement came from the man's brown hair as it shifted in the breeze.

Looking away, Mary found herself facing the stairs that led to her bedchamber. Raising her eyes, she made her decision and strode down the passage.

The bedchamber would have been in complete darkness had it not been for the solitary window above Mary's bed. Mary retrieved food and water from the little storage cupboard that sat in the one darkened corner of the room.

Maybe I shouldn't follow the same plan; Prater would know I had something to do with it before. No, it would be better to just follow the tunnel and enter when it is dark, wouldn't it? Mary's hand hovered in the air as she considered the thoughts.

Mary didn't want to raise Prater's suspicions, and she conceded he wouldn't be so careless again, but she would need to move quickly to ensure the dragon's survival.

After she placed the food back into the cupboard, Mary made her way downstairs and into the hidden room. She remained there until she felt the chill that came as darkness fell over the village. With a final glance back at the closed door to the book building, she started down the tunnel with a single candle to light the stone walls once the torches glow faded away.

At the end of the tunnel, Mary pressed her ear against the wall, listening for the slightest sound. She knew that they checked the prisoners regularly, and as Mary sat there, she heard the door to the cell open.

"All's well, Prater," Delwyn said, and Mary heard the door close again, scraping along the stone floor.

The time had come. She pressed the lever and reached through to place the candleholder on the floor just as she had the first time. As she climbed through the hole, she had the key in her hand ready. The dragon sat on the side where Michael had been, his eyes barely open. Mary placed her finger on her lips to elicit the dragon's silence, and he nodded in acknowledgment.

Putting the key in the handcuff, Mary attempted to turn it. It wouldn't budge. Panicking, her hands shook as she looked at the dragon. His blue-green eyes stared back at her momentarily before nodding back towards his wrist.

She tried the key again. This time Mary heard the click and closed her eyes in relief. Within moments she had freed him, but he didn't move. The weakened dragon appeared drained from the contact with gold, and Mary wondered how long Prater had held the dragon before returning to Tiani. Michael had been weak, but nothing compared to this man – no doubt remained in Mary's mind that sixteen was the correct number.

Mary helped him stand and they made their way to the door in the wall. His body shook as he began to go through the hole. He paused halfway through to catch his breath. Mary followed and felt relief as she pressed down on the lever to conceal the escape.

"The candle," hissed the dragon, and Mary reached to snatch it back just in time. She fell backwards with the candle in hand as the wall closed just as the cell door opened.

Mary froze with fear on the floor. Her breath caught in her throat at the thought of discovery. She couldn't be sure that the candle, or even she, hadn't been seen, or perhaps if the sound of the bricks had been heard…

"Prater, he's gone!" Delwyn yelped.

"What!" Prater's voice boomed through the wall.

Though Mary couldn't see the dragon, she heard him take in a sharp breath that he didn't release immediately. The wall they were leaning against shook as the cell door connected with it, followed by heavy footsteps over the stone floor.

"Get some light in here! Now!" Prater ordered.

"He's gone," the guard repeated as if he still couldn't believe his own words.

"I can see that he's gone! I'm not blind! Find him!"

Behind her, Mary felt the unfamiliar closeness of the dragon's body against hers. She hadn't been so close to anyone else in a long time, and she cringed at his warm breath on her ear. His hands on her arms restricted her from moving, but she couldn't seem to get him to loosen his grip. With her eyes closed, she counted the seconds until she could freely move.

Finally, the voices quieted in the room. Mary attempted to stand, but the dragon's hand tugged on her sleeve, and she took that as a sign that it wasn't yet safe to move. Mary wondered if perhaps the dragon could sense Prater on the other side, standing still in the cell, hoping to solve the puzzle. If they suspected a tunnel, they would destroy the cell to find it, and no doubt would remain of Mary's involvement. She shook the vision from her mind and focused on breathing to remain calm.

Another deep breath; Mary closed her eyes for a moment. The dragon still held onto her arm and at least their bodies protected each other from the cold. After a while, Mary's body felt cramped from the lack of movement. Her eyes had watched the candle as it burnt down to nothing, leaving them in darkness. The thought of making the journey back to the book building without light meant it would be slow. Still, the notion didn't linger long as the darkness had made her tired and she slipped into sleep.

Opening her eyes, the darkness confused Mary at first. She felt like she had slept the night away, but the lack of light made her feel she had woken in the middle of the night. She could hear nothing but the sound of her own regular breathing and that of the dragon's irregular breathing behind her.

Mary couldn't tell whether he was asleep or awake, but his hold had loosened so she took the opportunity to put some distance between them. As her hands felt for the familiar rough stone texture, she heard movement as the dragon stood behind her. His hand found her shoulder, and she pushed through her feelings to act as his guide, reminding herself that she should have good luck in her life now that she had truly saved a dragon's life.

Mary had walked the tunnels a hundred times over the years, but things were different without that one sense she relied upon. As she fumbled down the tunnel, Mary felt like the blind man in the neighbouring village that the children teased and threw things at because they knew he could do nothing to stop them. Even though the impairment would not last, Mary knew she didn't like the feeling of being without it, even for just that journey.

Despite any reservations she had, they soon saw the glow of light as they neared the lit end of the tunnel where the torches still burned. Once in the hidden room, the dragon sat on the bed, appearing completely exhausted as he rubbed his eyes.

"I'll get you fresh food and water." Mary bent down to pick up a clean plate from the shelf below the tabletop.

"Thank you," the dragon spoke his first words to her.

She didn't meet his face; she wanted to keep a firm emotional and physical distance between them now that they were safe.

"I'll bring some water so you can wash." Mary left him alone in the room.

Upstairs, Mary went to the front door where the sunshine flowed through the glass. People appeared to be going about their normal routines. Searching the faces, she couldn't find Prater or any of his loyal men. She didn't feel relieved at all at not finding him. Mary thought it most important to know where people were that you didn't want to find you.

In her bedchamber, Mary washed and put on her plain brown dress. In the reflection board, she caught a glimpse of the girl who stood facing her and then turned away. Picking up a cloth, she draped it over the board. She didn't need a reflection to mock her anymore. She headed downstairs to the main floor.

Mary went out the front door and strode over to the well where she drew up a bucket of fresh water. She could see a few of the men in their workshops already at work, but women and children were nowhere. Outside by the well, the town looked even eerier than what she had seen from her bedchamber's window. The smothering silence felt like a bad omen.

With her bucket filled, Mary returned to the book building and secured the front door behind her before double checking the bolt. She headed for the hidden room and found the dragon still there, sitting on the bed, looking weak but more alert.

With the bucket of water on the floor, Mary picked up an empty bowl from the floor beside the fireplace and gave it a quick wipe before refilling it and placing it on the table by the bed. The dragon caught her hand as she began to move away, and she jumped.

"You're bound?" His tone conveyed his surprise.

Mary tried to cover the back of her hand and inwardly cursed herself for overlooking her gloves. Her heart raced at the thought that anyone could have seen it while she had been at the well. His hand still held her fingers though.

"Yes," she replied, staring at the water in the bowl as the small ripples settled, and then added, "I am...I was...I..."

"Sorry." He held her hand a moment longer before letting it go, busying himself by picking up the cloth.

Mary retreated upstairs to prepare the food, but saw no point putting on the gloves now that he knew. The dragon would know that she wouldn't be after him as a husband and that he had no obligation to her beyond thanks.

"Pull yourself together!" Mary chastised herself as she cut the bread, but despite her firm resolve she couldn't stop the tears that fell from her eyes.

Taking a deep breath, Mary paused in her cutting to wipe the tears away with the back of her hand. She couldn't explain her sudden upsurge in emotion – it just wasn't normal. As she continued to cut, she lamented on how different things could have been if there hadn't been a leak in the ceiling, if the book hadn't been placed at the end of the shelf, if only she hadn't presumed that the number was... if...if...if – why?

After several minutes, she composed herself enough to take the food downstairs to the dragon.

Mary could see that he had washed, and though she didn't know for sure, she suspected that he had transformed into his dragon form due to the warmth in the room. People thought of dragons as huge creatures, but they weren't, according to the books. The dragons were said to be no more than twice the size as a dragon as they were in human form. In one book, Mary had seen the drawings of baby dragons and how cute and harmless they looked.

"Here's some food. You'll need to stay here until things quieten down out there." Mary turned to leave.

"Wait, won't you eat with me? There's plenty here."

Looking at the floor, she shook her head.

"It's the least I can do for you in return."

He seemed so gentle, so caring, it made Mary feel all the worse for the decision she had made. No, not the decision, the *mistake* she had made. Glancing towards the door, Mary searched her brain for a suitable reply so that she could return to the books.

"You've said thank you; that's all I need."

"No, I must pay you back. What's your name?" When Mary didn't reply, the dragon continued, "I'm Quinn."

"Mary."

As much as she tried to avoid looking at him, it proved difficult to do when talking. His pale brown skin indicated that he was from the north – close to the sea where the people with the white skin lived. Flowing brown hair framed his handsome face and the lovely blue-green eyes that reminded Mary of a painting in the main book room. The painting was of some size and hung above the main fireplace; it was of the ocean, something that Mary had never seen, but it seemed like such a wondrous part of nature in the painting, calm and vast with no beginning and no end.

"Whatever you want, just name it."

She closed her eyes, suppressing a wave of tears.

"There's nothing you can give me that I want. Please eat." Mary departed, and then entered the main book room, grateful for the solitude.

Standing with books all around and the fire burning did not lift Mary's low spirits. She had often wondered if books could be enough for her – just as they had been for Yansa. When he had passed, the enjoyment she had revelled in with each new book had faded away without the joy of someone to share

it with. Mary looked at her binding mark again, and
as her heart fell, so did her tears.

After the night Quinn thanked Mary, she tried her best to avoid going to the hidden room as much as possible. She didn't want to look at Quinn, she didn't want to get to know him – in fact, as far as Mary was concerned, the sooner that Quinn left the sooner Mary's life could return to "normal".

As Mary walked down the stone stairs with fresh linen, she hesitated just before the door. Something seemed different, something she couldn't put her finger on. Momentarily she stood there doing nothing but listening, wondering – while there seemed nothing to hear, her mind found plenty to wonder about.

Pushing the thoughts away, she continued into the room and saw Quinn seated. He glanced up as she entered and smiled. Mary tried to determine if he or anything else in the room looked different, but nothing stood out.

"Is everything alright?" Quinn asked, and Mary eyed him.

Has he just been a dragon and transformed back to a human?

"Fine," she replied.

The flames burned low but merry in the fireplace. She had been careful to avoid being seen collecting too much wood. The chimney of the hidden and narrow rooms backed onto each other and connected into one single chimney – otherwise a second chimney on that side would have been necessary and would look suspicious coming up from the ground without a purpose.

"What do you do here? Wherever here is."

Mary glanced in the direction he gestured before she returned her gaze to him. She contemplated whether to tell him the truth.

"The books. I'm the book-keeper."

A realisation passed over the dragon's face, and he smiled at Mary. "I'm in a book building, of course, that makes sense. Here let me let help you."

He moved towards her, stretching out his hands. Mary felt his hand brush against hers as he took the linen and moved away again. Her other hand rubbed the spot of contact as it tingled slightly.

"Is that why you saved me?"

"What do you mean?" Mary inquired, wanting to know what that mind of his had come up with first before saying anything that she might regret.

"Did you save me because of something you read?"

"Yes."

At least that's the truth, sort of. If he hadn't been a dragon I wouldn't have bothered, but I don't need any more bad luck.

Quinn stood beside the bed, and Mary glanced at the linen. Moving towards the pile at the end of the bed, she began unfolding one of the sheets. Picking it up to shake it, the cuff of her sleeve rose away from her wrist.

A hand reached out and touched hers. Mary froze as Quinn stepped closer. She wanted to pull her hand free and leave but felt stuck on the spot. His thumb traced over the mark.

"I know you said you were, but that binding mark is really fresh."

"I have work to do upstairs," Mary replied shortly, averting her gaze.

"The binding mark is fresh, Mary."

"Yes, it is." Mary again broke eye contact.

"But you said 'was' but the mark…" Quinn paused.

Mary shifted her feet and shook her head. "It's complicated."

Mary looked up at Quinn only to find him looking back her and not the mark. The truth of the binding continued to torment her; who would openly want to admit that they were bound to someone who had gone to continue their life elsewhere? She could have tried to lie about the binding mark, but anyone could tell he lived; the marks only disappeared when one part of the union died. When she had visited book buildings in the past, she'd heard the whispers about how dragons and sorcerers could break bindings but for a price she had no means to pay.

"Complicated?" Quinn released her hand and she placed the sheet back on the bed. "Binding to someone shouldn't be complicated…well, I guess there are some circumstances that might be, but really, they should be straightforward."

"I don't want to talk about it."

"It makes you sad thinking about it?"

Mary stole a glance and saw he continued to watch her. "Yes."

"Is it the reason you saved me from that cell? I'm fairly certain he had plans to hang me, if you hadn't have done what you did, I wouldn't be here now."

"Partly the reason. Like I said, it's complicated."

Mary felt relief at the greater distance between them as he moved towards the fire. Her hands smoothed out the crease in the sheet, but she still felt drawn to turn and watch him.

"Everything happens for a reason, Mary. That's what I believe anyway. We all have secrets; you can trust me, it's not like I can tell anyone while I'm here anyway."

"I can't tell you. It isn't just my secret." Their eyes met as he stared at her across the room; she tried to maintain the eye contact. "Plus, perhaps it would be better for you to know as little as possible."

"I don't see why," he pushed. Mary's hand abandoned the sheet and her feet were keen to head for the door. "What will you do once I'm gone?"

She nodded towards the entrance of the hidden room, "The books, they're all I have, and maybe this is just where I'm meant to be after all."

"I've heard it's a noble thing to do, caring for the books," Quinn said and stood up.

Mary tried to discern any hidden meaning in his words. *Does this mean my good luck will begin again?* "Yes, plus, I enjoy reading the books, but tomorrow you must leave."

"I'm not ready to go, not yet." Quinn replied, breaking eye contact and moving back towards the bed. He picked up the linen, placing it on a chair.

Mary stared at him as she took the linen off the bed and replaced it with the fresh ones she had brought down. Her mouth constantly tried to find things to say but she couldn't seem to verbalise them. She wondered if telling a dragon what to do would be a wise thing given the circumstances.

Once Quinn had smoothed the blanket down, he got comfortable on the bed, stretching out and casually interlocking his hands together behind his head.

"But you will need to leave. Prater is still looking for you, and I don't want..."

"Mary, I'm not ready to go yet."

Mary wondered if he could see the annoyance on her face. "No one will recognise you now."

She referred to the fact that he shaved his face which had changed his appearance dramatically –he now looked a ten years younger than when he had been in the cell. For a moment Mary tried to work out Quinn's age. He looked older than her but not as old as Prater.

"I need my strength, Mary. My home is a long way from here, and I am still very weak."

"If you are not from here, then why did you come?" Mary paused, her curiosity piqued, and she moved back towards the bed. It had been the one thing not mentioned in the book; it only predicted the dragon passing through the village but never gave any indication as to why. She had considered that maybe the dragon came purely to spread good luck but that had seemed unlikely given the recent history of Tiani and dragons.

Quinn leaned forward, his hands pushing on the bed, so he sat more upright, "I was searching for…my…brother…Jack. He left some weeks ago and hasn't returned home, I just want to know that he is safe and well."

"Maybe by now he has returned home?" Mary suggested as she sat down at the end of the bed, trying to sound hopeful and convince him that a quick return would be best.

"Maybe, but at least even if he hasn't returned, I will still be able to let...let my family know," Quinn paused and looked over at Mary. "Where are your parents?"

Her face fell at the question and she looked at her hands that sat in her lap. "Dead."

"Oh, I'm sorry."

Mary shrugged her shoulders and spoke evenly, "It isn't your fault – it's Prater's fault solely. If he hadn't tried to...never mind, it's all in the past now anyway."

"He tried to do something?"

"He angered the dragons."

"Ah, did he try to destroy the books? To burn the books?"

Mary gripped her hands together and began to wring them. "Yes, when I was six."

"Books are sacred to dragons. They have protected them throughout time for a reason."

They? Why wasn't he saying we?

"Why not just destroy Prater though? Why did so many have to die?" Mary felt this would be her only opportunity to get some kind of answer about why her family had to die, why she had to grow up without them.

"Because there will always be another Prater. It sends a message. The curse of death on the books has been there for longer than I have been alive. Dragons can't lift or change it – it is just how things are with the dragon magic that was used." His sentences were misleading. The way he spoke sounded like he was talking about someone, something, else.

Then again, Mary thought to herself, *what reason did he have to tell me the truth – me, a foolish, plain village human girl whom nobody cares about?*

Mary looked towards the door. It wasn't the answer she wanted, but then again, she really didn't know what she wanted to know anymore. No matter what the reasons behind the curse, knowing them wouldn't bring her family back.

If the binding had taught her anything, it was that books could be very dangerous, or at least misleading, with the knowledge they contained. She rebuked herself for not listening to Yansa's advice. If he had lived longer, she wondered if he would have eventually explained his warning about that one particular book especially. Mary knew Yansa probably only intended to shield her from making mistakes, but it seemed to her that telling her might have prevented some of her poor decisions.

"I'd best go back upstairs," Mary said as she stood and started towards the door.

Quinn quickly got up from his relaxed pose on the bed and stood as well, catching her hand in his momentarily. "Give it another week, Mary, maybe by then I will be strong enough to leave."

She nodded reluctantly and left the room. As she walked up the steps to the bookcase entrance, Mary could feel the warmth on her hand from where Quinn had touched her, like a match that burns hot, then warm, and then dissipates as if it never existed.

CHAPTER SEVEN

Quinn had been in Tiani for a couple of weeks, and Mary felt a sense of urgency to get Quinn home. She had resolved that he needed to go before the whispers from the villagers that the dragon had remained close prompted anyone to look too closely her way.

In the village, Mary kept to her usual routine and listened for news of Prater. He and his men had been gone for over a week, and an uneasy tension hung over the village. Mary didn't know for sure, but she suspected that she wasn't the only one in the village with a poor opinion of Prater. Yet the regular sense of protection and safety felt absent from Tiani since Prater had left.

Mary turned around in the main book room, watching as the fire slowly died down to nothing. She had tidied up the few books she had removed from shelves but still held one in her hand that she had planned to read for a bit before sleeping. As she walked towards the staircase though, she hesitated; she didn't feel sleepy in the slightest, and the quietness of the book building amplified her sense of loneliness.

Her eyes travelled until they found the bookcase in the narrow book room. *A little company would be welcome.* She had found herself spending much of her spare time with Quinn reading and talking about books, and it had reminded her of how much she loved reading and sharing what she'd read.

Smoothing her hair down with her hands, Mary headed for the hidden room. There she found Quinn looking at one of the books she had left there earlier in the day. He looked over it as she entered the room.

"It's interesting."

Mary smiled. "I always found that one a bit boring myself. The language is much older, and it makes it difficult to read." She had chosen it thinking that he would appreciate a book on his dragonkind.

"It mentions a bit about the Great War."

"Yeah, it has a little in it, but it's not really detailed enough to understand about what happened to cause it all, or how it was resolved for that matter."

"So, all you know about the Great War is in these books?"

"Yes, we don't have any other books about it in our collection, but some of the larger book buildings do – at least that's what Yansa told me," Mary paused and looked over at the man. "I suppose it didn't tell you anything new?"

He smiled and nodded. "I know more than what this book has. It's a bit vague to be honest. I'm wondering if it was written by a human."

"I guess you know all about it then?"

"Kind of difficult to avoid the topic growing up." Quinn looked over at Mary. "You want to hear about it?"

"Sure." Mary smiled at the thought of learning something new that wasn't from a book. She settled into the chair near the fire so she could distract her attention if necessary.

"I'll be honest, I'm not sure how much is actually factual and how much is embellished so just keep that in mind. The legend goes though that a long time ago, dragons, sorcerers, and humans all lived separately in their own kingdoms and were restricted to them. As time passed, a disease began to spread through the dragon territory – it was devastating. This disease destroyed the plants and poisoned the water. Many dragons died and even more fell ill for long periods of time.

No one knew what had caused it, but an older dragon called Miffen accused a sorcerer of creating the disease to try and wipe out all dragons. That sorcerer was a High Sorcerer called Illya, the one in charge of the kingdom, and he denied the charge."

"Had he though, the sorcerer?"

Quinn shrugged. "At first, no one believed the disease existed but then the dragons started moving north into the human's kingdom. Only then did Illya send sorcerers into the old dragon kingdom to assess if the disease existed. When the sorcerers reported the disease was real and reported on the damage it had caused. Illya had stated he wanted to see if anything could be done to fix the area for the dragons to return to their territory and journeyed there himself. The dragons, you see, had warned all sorcerers to stay away from their kingdom. Of course, when Illya reached the land he said that what he saw was a land regenerating. That's when some of the dragons accused him of causing the damage since the land only appeared to recover once Illya went there. Miffen led the dragons, vowing to get revenge on Illya and all sorcerers."

Mary leaned forward. "So what happened?"

"Nothing at first, but then the humans also saw that the land was healthy, and with the dragons in their kingdom, some humans moved south. Around that time, a younger dragon, an apprentice of Miffen's, became bound to a human, and it had…unexpected consequences." Quinn looked over at Mary as she watched him intently.

"Good luck?"

"Sort of," Quinn hesitated. "A long time had passed since the dragon's moving out of their kingdom, long enough that humans and dragons co-existed. Many dragons lived their lives in human form, while others chose to live in dragon form in the mountains beyond the Great Forest. I suppose it was only a matter of time before two would fall in love."

"What about the sorcerers? Did they…mingle as well?"

Quinn leaned forward and shook his head, "Not as much. Most sorcerers chose to live in magical homes. So, they do have a physical access point, but basically the house exists on another, I'm not sure how to explain it, but maybe like a magical bubble hidden away from this world. Some sorcerers did spread out though, but the Sorcery Council formed and advised that they stayed put."

"So, if the human got luck from binding to a dragon, what's the big deal?"

"The luck runs both ways, and it's not luck as such, not really, it's… For example, when a pure-human, so one with no sorcerer or dragon blood, binds to a magical being – dragon or sorcerer – the magic becomes ten times more powerful."

"But that doesn't make sense. I mean there were so many humans…"

"It was thought that the kingdoms had always been separate, but given that many humans have traces of sorcerer or dragon blood, some both, it means that some time, way before things were recorded in books, there must have been a time when everyone lived assimilated."

"So, this human then?"

"Had neither dragon nor sorcerer blood; that's what made the union powerful. When Miffen realised this, he launched an attack on Illya while he felt the power favoured the dragons."

"The Great War?"

"Yeah. Illya bound to a pure-human as well, and the war went on for a long time. In the end, both lost their partners in the war on the same day. Some say that the humans took their own lives to stop the war, but, well, I guess no one will ever know for sure. The two sides agreed to a truce but also a set of rules that both dragons and sorcerers had to abide by.”

“Including not binding to a human?”

“Yeah, it's a blanket rule of humans in general, but the real concern is a pure-human. I mean back then pure-humans were more common.”

Mary looked at her binding mark; she hadn't considered there might have been any rules. Being bound to a dragon had seemed the easiest way to secure the good luck long term and start a new life somewhere other than Tiani. *But it seems that would not have been possible anyway.*

“What are you thinking?”

Mary raised her eyes. “That it seems like power destroyed the balance more than once in the history of the kingdoms.”

“Yeah, I guess power is a tempting for some people.”

“Not you?”

The laughter took Mary by surprise. He shook his head. “No, the pursuit of power is something...something that's impacted my life too much.”

"You just want to return to…" Mary let the sentence hang, not knowing if he preferred human or dragon form.

"Just return home."

"Once you find your brother?"

"Who? Oh yeah, once I find him again."

Mary's hand gripped the book.

Quinn glanced at it. "Is that a new one for me?"

"Oh, I was going to read it…it's about wildflowers. When it's warm here, there are a few places where they grow just inside the Great Forest. You're probably not interested in reading about flowers though."

"Beauty always interests me."

Mary glanced up at him and she felt her heart skip. A smile crept onto her face as she opened the book to a random page.

Quinn patted the bed. "Be easier to see if you sit beside me."

Mary moved over and sat beside him on the bed, trying to focus on the illustration of a dragon rose as Quinn moved closer. She could feel the warmth along the side of her leg where their bodies met. His finger tapped on the blue rose.

"You know, I saw a red and blue one once. The centre was this vibrant type of blue, but it blended with a dark red along the edge of the petals. I never saw another one like that though, most are only one colour."

"Sometimes, just before the snow comes, we get white ones growing near the bridge."

"Mary?"

"Yes?" She purposely didn't look at Quinn. Her feelings were clear to her now. She liked being around Quinn, reading with him, talking to him.

"Are you happy staying here? With the books?"

"I love my books."

"Yeah, I know, but sometimes you need to leave things you love in order to live."

Mary watched Quinn's hand move away from the rose and back to her hand.

"Is there somewhere else you'd rather be? Someone else?"

Mary swallowed, feeling herself on the verge of confessing all. "This is my home, Quinn," she whispered.

"That's avoiding answering my question, Mary. You should be around other people closer to your own age, be around people who share your love of reading and books."

"I..." Mary paused at a familiar sound, muffled through the doors and walls, but still she heard it. "I need to go, someone's at the door."

"Mary." He still held her hand as she stood to go.

"Tomorrow, Quinn, tomorrow."

CHAPTER
EIGHT

Back upstairs, Mary stoked the fire in the narrow room as she passed through it. The flames crackled beneath the wood before emerging to engulf it. Mary pulled her shawl tight over her shoulders, noting that she had felt warmer while downstairs with Quinn.

Another knock at the door demanded Mary's attention, and she took a deep breath. Her heart still beating wildly in her chest, she stood up and smoothed the skirt of her dress down. Tucking a few loose strands of hair behind her ears, she slowly exhaled the breath she had been holding, pulling the shawl closer around her shoulders to fend off the cold air as she walked towards the passage.

She glanced at the glowing lantern that lit the way, thankful she hadn't put it out before going to see Quinn. As she drew near the entrance, she saw Prater through the window in the door. Her heart fell and she swallowed nervously before licking her lips.

Turning the handle, Mary could feel her hand shaking. She tried to soothe her nerves by taking a deep breath so the fear wouldn't be heard in her voice when she spoke. *My hand, where is my glove?* She shoved her left hand into the pocket of her apron. She opened the door, relieved that Prater had been talking to his men or he would have surely seen the mark through the glass.

"Hello, Mary," Prater said as he pushed the door open, forcing her to take a step back as he invited himself into the book building. His men remained at the foot of the steps, waiting for their cue. Mary ignored the men and focused on Prater.

"Hello, Master Prater," Mary replied as evenly as she could. In her pocket, her hand fidgeted with the material of her apron.

"I heard that you had returned from a trip…" His eyes glanced at her uncovered right hand with suspicion written all over his face, "…I heard your hands had been burnt."

"Just my left hand, Master, hot water spilled – I wasn't paying enough attention…" Mary tried to jam her hand further into her pocket as she rambled on, knowing that she was saying too much about the supposed accident, "I...I...I didn't know you had returned."

Prater inclined his head to one side as Mary shuffled her soft shoes across the stone floor. She hated that his gaze didn't shift away from her face.

"I didn't know you were paying such close attention to my movements." Prater winked at Mary and she quickly turned away. She bit her lip hard enough to draw blood as she felt an involuntary blush spread across her cheeks. "I only returned a few moments ago...I need to look around. All the buildings are being searched. The dragon can't be far as we know he hasn't yet left the area." Prater's eyes finally broke the gaze on Mary's face and began darting around the passage room like an eagle seeking its prey.

"How can you be sure?"

Prater waved at his men, and Mary watched as they walked past and entered the main book room. She heard a few thuds and looked in the direction to try and see what they were doing, but she couldn't escape from Prater's presence.

"Because our crops are still failing, Mary. I saw it with my own eyes as I rode back into town."

Trapped behind the door, Mary frantically glanced around, looking for a way out of the situation. Prater still held the door ajar with his right hand, standing so close Mary could feel his breath on her face as he leaned down. With nowhere to go, Mary's eyes fell back on Prater. His head moved to the side as his cold eyes continued to watch her.

"You don't mind if I look around too, do you?"

"Go ahead, Master," she replied reluctantly. If she'd owned the building maybe she might have been able to refuse but it belonged to the village.

Prater smiled as he nudged the door closed. She watched as he pushed off the wall and sauntered over to the entrance of the main room. He stood there casually looking around while Mary stared down at the floor with contempt. In her mind she imagined his face down there and her foot itched to stamp on it.

Now she had steadied herself against the wall, Mary took a deep breath. With her eyes closed, she could hear Prater's footsteps on the stone floor in the main room. Another breath. Mary forced herself to take the few steps needed to see Prater. She watched as he walked from table to table, scowling at the piles of books that were upon them.

Excusing herself, Mary hurriedly made her way up the stairs to her bedchamber and put on the gloves, thankful for the small protection they offered. Not wanting him to think her a suspect in the dragon's disappearance, she returned downstairs to find Prater still there, but he wasn't searching like his men were, just standing there, watching his men do all the work.

Even though Mary knew he would not find the dragon, she was feeling cautious, nervous. Mary had always felt Prater was conceited and too sure of himself. She'd often wondered if growing up without siblings explained why he put himself above others and made others do what he wanted. She had once read a passage in a book that said sorcerers were sneaky, would bully others to do their bidding, and were obnoxious – Mary considered Prater might be one then since he held all the necessary traits. Yansa had always insisted that claims should have more than one source to be considered accurate, but detailed information about sorcerers had proven to be elusive.

She watched as the men looked under tables, behind doors, in cupboards, and watched as row after row of books were tossed from the shelves and onto the ground. Mary consigned herself to the reality that the better part of her day would be taken up by the search, and she had no way of warning

Quinn who was safely tucked away in the hidden room.

Sitting down at a table, Mary moved the brown-covered book on dragons to the bottom of another pile of books in case Prater saw the engraved dragon on the cover. She picked up an innocent book on crops that she didn't feel like reading at that moment but felt it probably could solve the issue of the failed crops. According to what she had read, plants could get sick the same as everything else; diseases could attack from the air or be drawn from the ground.

Looking up she wanted to say something. *He's never going to listen to me though.*

The men and Prater moved into the narrow room, and Mary felt a small burst of relief knowing that they shouldn't notice the lever, at least she hoped not. It seemed like a long while before she looked up and Prater was standing in the doorway, obviously having finished his search. The look on his face however remained, even when he saw that Mary had noticed his presence. She began to feel uncomfortable under his gaze.

"Have you finished searching then?" Mary asked, interrupting the silence and hoping to break his gaze as well. It didn't work.

"We have finished the search." Prater's men started to return to the main room, and he nodded them towards the door.

Mary was alternating her gaze between Prater and his men, until only he stood there with her.

"At least for the moment we have."

Mary closed the book in her hand, but he made no move to follow his men out.

"We've both lived in this village a long time, Mary."

"We were both born here."

Staring at the cover of the crop book, she heard his footsteps as he walked over to the table that she sat at. She tapped her fingers nervously on the cover of the book and tried to find something, anything, to focus her attention on.

"You should have been bound by now, Mary, like the other couple of girls in the village are."

"There are no more unbound men in the village." Mary regretted the words immediately.

Mary shifted in her seat; she had the feeling this conversation might be revisiting their earlier one on the walk. She rubbed the back of her hand against the pocket fabric as if the mark could be erased so easily.

"I'm still unbound, Mary." He leaned over the desk, and she looked up to find the same look on his face as before in the passage. "I spent so long keeping control of this village, I never stopped to think about binding – not until recently really."

Maybe there were some advantages to Michael having come to the village after all, Mary thought. She did not know how to respond to his words though and her feet shifted nervously beneath the table.

"Maybe I should now. What do you think, Mary?"

"About what, Master Prater?" Mary wanted to move the chair back and away from him. Her attention had been on the cover of the book for too long to keep staring at it. She picked up another book about bridges.

"You and me, Mary."

She bit her lower lip hard and tasted the blood.

"Think about it, Mary."

Her eyes swept over the desk before she looked up and their eyes met. He reached over and touched the side of her face, smiling before he straightened up and left the main room.

Then, just when she felt relief that he appeared to be leaving, he turned around. His brows were furrowed, and his gaze focused on the book in her hand while he sneered. "Why do you bother with those things? They are of no good to anyone, Mary."

Mary put down the book in her hand and looked up at him annoyed. Books still had value in her eyes. She knew the mistake had been hers and not the book's fault. Her hand reached back for the original book she had in her hand. "This book is about crops, Master. Maybe it has an answer in it to explain why the crops are failing…"

"It's the dragon, Mary, the dragon that is responsible for the crops!"

Startled by the sudden outburst, Mary reminded herself that his temper was one of the reasons she would never want to bind to him. Yansa had said repeatedly that he never wanted to see Prater bound, and the older Mary grew the more she understood why Yansa felt that way. There had been times when Mary thought the dragons had granted his wish in return for trying to warn Prater about burning the books.

"Yes, Master," her reply was weak and quiet. She wanted him to leave her alone.

"Mary, the sooner you realise that we are all better off without books, the better off you will be as well. We could simply lock the door. The books will remain here. The information they contain is worthless to us. Think about my offer." He said nothing more to Mary as he turned and left her home.

A few moments after the footsteps had faded away, Mary rose, and once at the door, decisively closed it before sliding the lock into place. Through the clear pane, Mary watched as Prater swaggered back over to the detention building while she turned the lock on the door to make sure no-one else would think there was an open invitation into the book building. Turning around, she yelped in surprise.

"Quinn!" Mary was annoyed he had managed to sneak up on her.

"I heard noise...and...a man raised his voice. I was concerned."

Mary grabbed Quinn's sleeve and pulled him further back into the corridor well away from the front door, though she doubted that anyone outside would have seen Quinn anyway. Still, Mary didn't want to take any chances.

"It was Prater; he knows that you are still here." Mary wanted Quinn to hear the pleading and urgency in her voice for him to leave. She wondered why she was so concerned to see Quinn safely away so quickly. This was no longer just about receiving good luck. She would have liked Quinn to stay forever, but he needed to be gone, not just so the good luck could keep flowing, but because she wanted to keep him safe.

Quinn smiled, seemingly unconcerned. "No, he believes that I haven't left the area, but he doesn't know I'm here. After all, didn't they just search the place?"

"Still, I think it would be safer if you left, safer for you." Mary grabbed Quinn's sleeve and tugged him in the direction of the room.

"I know you're right," he paused and looked searchingly into Mary's face. He placed his hand over hers on his sleeve. "Will you come with me?"

"And what would I do?" Mary replied jokingly to avoid answering the question

"Stay with me as my guest. We can continue our conversations, and you can have as many books as you like," Quinn half-smiled as he said it. His eyes watched her a little too much, and she turned around so his gaze didn't capture her soul completely.

"I think I'd become bored very quickly." Mary's hand itched, and she began to remove her glove before stopping herself. Curling her fingers tighter around the woollen material, she found herself pulling the glove on tighter than before. "Anyway, there are the books...no one else in this village will see to their care...and really it is my duty...to Yansa...and the dragons...and really, taking care of the books is not a bad thing to do. After all, there is plenty to do...or read..."

Mary heard him take a step closer behind her, and she felt his hand on her right shoulder, "Mary..."

Moving away, she shrugged his hand off, and her mild tone melted away like a glacier into the ocean, "Quinn, you must leave and return to your home. Tiani is not a safe place for a dragon to be."

"A dragon?"

Turning, Mary glanced over at him. He gazed at her with a playful look in his eyes and a smile on his lips. She quickly averted her gaze to a pile of books that she felt needed her attention.

"I'll leave tomorrow night," he said in defeat. "But Mary, until then, my offer stands."

Mary heard his footsteps fade behind her but then pause, and she knew he needed her help to return to the safety of the hidden room. The truth was out there now, and Mary felt content knowing Quinn knew she recognised him as being a dragon.

CHAPTER NINE

A tremendous thud shook Mary awake as the sounds from downstairs echoed up to her bedchamber. Hurriedly, Mary put on her plain brown dress and rushed down to the floor below. The door to the book building rested on the ground surrounded by the glass that had shattered over the stone floor. It pained her to think about how to get that fixed or how she might pay for it. She looked out through the void, in the distance could see the hanging tree beyond the well. Tearing her gaze away from the tree, she saw Prater standing amongst the devastation, ordering men to do his bidding. He paused when he saw Mary standing in the doorway of the main room.

"Good morning, Mary," he said in the same way he might have greeted her in the street.

"What's going on?" she said, trying not to sound too demanding, but she felt angry about the search, especially so soon after the last. "The dragons won't be happy about this, they will be angry that you are damaging the books, preventing me from caring for them."

"We're just doing another search, Mary, it's not like we're burning the books or anything like that."

Mary sighed in frustration at Prater's response. He sauntered towards her from where he had been standing. His eyes narrowed on Mary as he took each step, and she could not maintain the gaze. Just centimetres away from Mary, Prater paused.

"Billy tells me he saw a man in here after I left yesterday – who would that be Mary?"

"Billy must have been mistaken – clearly I'm the only one here." Her words didn't have the confident ring to it she had hoped.

"Don't play games with me, Mary; the man was seen here – *he* must be the reason you are hesitating on my offer. Would being bound to me be so bad?"

Mary wanted to shout in his face that she would rather die first, but his men were already turning over tables and pulling all the books off their shelves. If Prater ordered, she could be hung before sunset.

"Master Prater, tell them to stop – there is no one else here!" Mary pleaded. It had taken her most of the night to put the books back on the shelves and she hardly wanted to have to shelve everything again.

Prater sneered before his hand reached out and grabbed Mary's right wrist. She tried to twist her hand away, but he held it firm as he removed her glove with his free hand. An abrupt change swept over Prater's face as his eyes found the binding mark.

"What's this?" he whispered; clearly he hadn't expected to see a binding mark. Mary gulped and tried to free her hand again as Prater leaned closer. When she failed to provide an explanation, his mouth curled into a snarl. "What is this, Mary?"

"A binding mark, Master, it's a binding mark." Mary's wrist ached from his hold and had begun to redden around the paleness of where he held her.

"When...who..." His questions faded off, and Mary tried to think quickly of an excuse.

"I was bound when I went to Haversy...to...to another book-keeper. He was here yesterday to see me..."

Prater moved closer to her; she tried to back away, but his hand held tightly onto her wrist. "If he was here yesterday, then why did we not find any sign of him?"

Good question. "He…he…he only arrived when you left."

"I saw no one enter the book building." His eyes narrowed on Mary; it wasn't the look that had covered his face the day before, but she didn't like it any better. "You're lying, Mary. You're not bound to a book-keeper…you're bound to the dragon, aren't you?" Prater's voice boomed in her face, and Mary found herself reeling backwards, tears moments from falling.

"No, I swear I'm not lying…" Mary claimed as she lost her balance and fell onto the hard, stone floor. Prater had stumbled forward but released her wrist in time to regain his footing. He loomed over her, casting his shadow across the light.

"Then why not say anything about the binding? Why conceal it with a lie? Why hide him? Why make a fool out of me?" Prater crouched in front of her.

Tears fell from her eyes despite her best attempts to prevent them. Memories of the burning flooded her mind and the same feeling swept through her body; she felt scared, powerless. Her lips trembled as they failed to find the right words.

Her body shook as she cowered from Prater. Her eyes darted trying to find an escape.

"I made her promise."

Both Prater and Mary turned as the soft tone interrupted the harsh interrogation. A beautiful woman stood behind Prater. Her red haired flowed loose around her shoulders and against her dark blue dress; her eyes were a piercing emerald green and her snow-white complexion soft and light against the darkness inside the book building.

"Don't be angry at her; I made Mary promise."

"And who are you?" Prater demanded.

The woman smiled and continued to capture Prater's own gaze with hers. She took a small, but purposeful, step towards Prater. Mary watched her feet as she moved yet again and noted that her step made no sound.

"I am her sister, by binding of course." She paused. "I made her promise because my brother is a very powerful man, and I didn't want him to feel too overwhelmed by the simple villagers." Again, she paused, as if on purpose. "Please release Mary's wrist."

Prater did as she requested immediately and stood up straight; his shadow still kept Mary in darkness but she appreciated the distance. Mary had no idea who the woman could be as she didn't look like Michael. The thought nagged away, making her nervous given the unusual events of the past couple of days.

"But book-keepers are not powerful…" Prater began, and the woman laughed the slightest of laughs. His jaw set as he scowled.

"Silly man, my brother is not a book-keeper."

Prater looked at Mary instead of the woman.

"Now please, order your men to leave immediately so that I may talk with my sister."

"Men, abandon everything where it is and leave."

Oooh, that's not normal behaviour, she is not a human at all. Mary's eyes followed the men as they marched stiffly past her and out of the building with Prater in tow; she pursed her lips before turning back to the woman. *There's only one explanation – she must be a sorceress.*

Alone with the unnamed woman, Mary felt small. Her heart beat hard in her chest and she felt sweat soaking into the gloves. As Mary watched the woman's face, the placid, sincere look altered to reveal a sneer.

"You stupid girl!" her voice cut through the newfound silence, and the dark blue colour of her dress darkened to black. Her voice sent a shockwave reverberating through the building.

"Excuse me?" Confusion consumed Mary and quickly mixed with her fear.

"I planned to be bound to Michael for years; years I slaved away to see my plan work, and then you, you stupid girl, you con him into becoming bound to you!"

"Michael?" Mary tried to think of some way to appease the woman. "I...I..."

"What, no answer?" The woman paced back and forth with her hands clenched by her side. "All my hard work!"

Suddenly, Mary found the woman's eyes focused back on her. A wave of fear swept over Mary – compared to this woman Prater seemed almost like an amateur at intimidation.

"There's nothing I can do..."

"You are bound to him! I can't even undo that – I, a powerful sorceress, can't do a thing about you since you're a human." She paused and looked Mary up and down. "I want to kill you, to break the binding spell, but that's not allowed either!"

Mary breathed in relief. *I guess in some ways mortal humans are more powerful.*

The woman took a step towards her and Mary swallowed hard, wondering if her magic allowed her to read private thoughts. The sorceress's eyes glared at her, and Mary felt the wall at her back as she attempted to move away.

"Yes, human, I am unable to kill you; it's against the rules, but you have no idea how big of a problem you created for me. Michael and I were to be bound next month and now I'm trapped in this nightmare of your creation. Perhaps I should turn you into an old woman...no, I have a better idea."

Mary warily glanced at her as the sorceress moved towards the table to her left. The desktop had books and papers in piles that she had been going through, trying to understand about soil and the weather and how they affect crops. The sorceress paused by one of the tables and her finger lightly traced the embossing on the top book.

"I didn't...I..."

The woman's eyes narrowed in on Mary, "You, a plain, simple little book-keeper thought that someone like Michael would want to be with you?" The laugh that escaped her lips sent chills both up and down Mary's spine before she looked away from the woman.

"Cecilia!"

Both Mary and the sorceress turned at the sound of Quinn' voice, not the soft voice Mary had become accustomed to but one much more forceful.

Does he know this woman?

Quinn's set face focused on the woman as he took a step towards the woman and stretched his left hand to her, "Don't do it, sister."

"Why not?" Cecilia had placed her hands on her hips and turned to face Quinn.

"Please sister, I beg of you..."

"I understand brother. It is fine for you to interfere with my business, but not the other way around?"

"This is between us Cecilia; it has nothing to do with Mary."

"It has everything to do with her! It is because of her that I have come here – I thought I only had to worry about you meddling in my business. I didn't think I needed to shield Michael from stupid village girls!"

"Mary's not..." Quinn started and a blue glow began to form around his hand.

Mary's eyes widened at the magic. *Sister, brother...glowing hands...if she's a sorceress then...*

"You're a sorcerer?" Mary whispered.

"Come on Cecilia, you owe Mary. She saved me sister; they had me bound in gold..."

"Then she should have left you to hang!"

"And Michael? If it wasn't for Mary, he would have hung too!" Quinn replied and Cecilia pursed her lips.

"How has that helped me at all – dead or alive I can't bind to him now!" Cecilia growled and took a step towards her brother. "Then what shall I do, brother? What would *you* have me do?"

"Leave Mary be."

"Leave her be?" Cecilia smiled at her brother. "Are you thinking of breaking the same rule you were preventing me from breaking? That's very bad of you brother."

Mary was only paying the slightest attention to them as she was battling her own inner voice: *The Golden Law. Why did I save a sorcerer? This is not going to bring me any luck; my luck might even get worse.* Her head shook in disbelief and her fingers grasped that fabric of her skirt. Tears welled in her eyes as her breathing quickened to match her racing heart.

"Cecilia…"

"I love you baby brother, despite all your faults and interference, however while the binding solved your task, I'm infuriated. I can't just let that go by; watch all my work and sacrifices – sacrifices that whether you believe it or not would have benefited you too." Cecilia paused and the corners of her mouth turned up. "I see all these books around and they're open, I think I am inspired."

Cecilia turned and walked back to where she had been standing first with a smile playing on her lips. Mary felt small, insignificant, cowering on the ground like a beaten dog. Mary hated hearing a conversation that she couldn't follow or understand; it made her feel stupid.

"You took what was mine, Mary, so I will take what you need and value the most."

Mary glanced at Quinn. A brief smiled flashed on Cecilia's lips as she raised her arms, but just as quickly vanished in a spray of blue light. Mary saw Quinn's arms fall to his side a moment before the world turned to darkness.

CHAPTER
TEN

"Mary, Mary," Quinn's hand shook her shoulder and when she turned to look at him, she could see the concern. "Are you alright?"

"I don't feel any different." Mary took a moment to glance around, everything looked the same. Despite her conviction that nothing was altered, she had a nagging feeling in the pit of her stomach; it insisted that something had changed but provided no more information. "You must leave Quinn; it's not safe for you to stay here."

"Are you sure? My sister, her curses and spells can be a bit unpredictable. It might be something small." Mary shook her head and sat up; looking beyond him at the books that covered the floor.

"Prater will return, Quinn. You really need to leave as..."

"But Mary..." Quinn began but Mary's attention had wandered.

She glanced around the corridor and to the broken door that lay on the floor, before landing back on the books strewn around the floor. The sight made her sad and she felt compelled to fix it as soon as possible; despite everything she didn't want to upset the dragons and bring any additional bad luck to her life.

"Quinn, and you must go back to your home...and be with your own kind. I need to deal with this." Her hands waved over the mess before them. "I only have my books left; I need to make sure that I don't lose that as well."

Quinn grabbed Mary's shoulders; he turned her so that she faced him, and she met his eyes for a moment. "Mary."

"I told you, Quinn, I'm perfectly okay. Nothing has changed. I must put the books away. The main room is a mess again."

"Mary, the books will remain with or without you to watch over them. You can't allow the books to control your life..."

Mary stood up, leaving Quinn kneeling on the stone floor in passage room. Her feet moved slowly as she walked into the main room and began to pick up the books one at a time. She didn't give them a second glance as she made piles to pick up and carry later. Until she saw a cover with a dragon.

Crouched down ready to grab the book, her hand hovered over it. Mary cocked her head to one side as if that would assist her, but nothing changed. Slowly she started shaking her head back and forth.

"No, no, no…"

Quinn joined her where she stood staring at the cover of the book. Quickly she picked up another and bit her lip as tears welled in her eyes.

"What's wrong?" he asked.

"I can't read the title. I don't understand…I can't read any more."

Mary's hands clasped together over her mouth as her own words repeated in her mind. Reading had been the only thing that had ever made her feel special instead of completely useless. *How can I take care of the books if I don't know what they are?*

"I'll fix it, Mary, I promise," Quinn said softly from behind her.

Mary turned, anger stirring inside her.

"You'll fix it? This is all your fault! You were meant to be a dragon, but instead you're a sorcerer.

I rescued a sorcerer!" Mary threw the book in his direction, though he only had to turn his body slightly to avoid being hit by it.

"Hey, it's not so bad..." Quinn said, putting a smile on his face as he stepped closer to Mary. "Look, maybe I should have told you that I wasn't a dragon when I realised, but you had your mind made up as to what I was. I thought you might turn me out, and I would have regretted that, having to leave on bad terms."

"Bad terms? I don't think lying is exactly the foundation of a friendship."

"I didn't lie though, Mary, not exactly. I just didn't correct your assumption. Mary..."

Shaking her head, Mary pointed her finger at Quinn, "First, I miscalculate and rescue Michael... *bind* to Michael; then I think I'll still have good luck simply rescuing a dragon...but I've made another mistake. The book was wrong!"

Quinn moved around so that he faced Mary once again. "What did the book tell you, Mary? Did it say there would be a *dragon*?"

Mary paused and thought back to the book. "It said a *good* powerful being...it had to be a dragon. Besides, the book was about dragons and not sorcerers. The books are written by dragons."

"Mary, dragons maintain the books, but many were written by humans and sorcerers as well."

"I have to believe what I was told Quinn. Despite everything that has happened with my family and life, I have to believe that dragons are *good* creatures."

"And sorcerers aren't?" Quinn countered defensively.

"Exactly!" Mary dropped the book in her hand to the ground. "The dragons took away any chance of luck that night of the burning. We were all punished because of what happened that night. The only way I can get some luck, some happiness coming back my way is to keep them happy. I maintain these books; I learn from what I read. I've done everything I can think of to be good, to appease the dragons. They're the only ones that can turn my luck around."

Quinn's eyebrows knitted. Reaching out, he gently touched Mary's cheek and ran his fingers down her face until he held her chin in his right hand between his thumb and index finger. He raised her face upwards so that her eyes were looking at him and not the discarded book.

Softly Quinn whispered to her, "Mary. Sorcerers aren't all bad, just like not all dragons are good. Dragon magic…"

"So why is it I am unable to read? That's not a *dragon's* fault –it's all a *sorcerer's* fault." Mary pushed his hand away, determined to keep her anger going. "And I got two-for-one today!"

"Mary, keep your voice down, someone may hear you." Quinn paused and looked around before adding, "Prater may hear you."

"Get out. You don't need me to help you, you can help yourself. You could have left at any time. You made a fool out of me!" She whipped around to face Quinn. Her anger bubbled over, expressing her frustration at losing her gift of reading and feeling betrayed by Quinn. While she didn't want to admit it aloud, a small part of her acknowledged the hurt Prater must have felt about her hiding the truth and the subsequent feeling of being a fool.

"Mary…"

"Just get out!"

"Mary, let me explain…"

"Get out!"

"Mary, I couldn't have just…"

"Leave me be."

"But Mary, let me explain first, please..."

Her head shook in response and he held his head in his hands for a moment.

Mary cast her gaze down at the book on the floor. It stared up at her, mocking her, like two girls whispering a secret that you would never hear yourself.

Picking up one book at a time, she placed them randomly back on the shelves–just to make the room look tidier. With certain books Mary felt frustrated as she recognised them; she looked at them once, twice, multiple times. All the books she wanted to read, she now couldn't. All the knowledge they contained lost as they would now sit idle on the shelves. Yansa had once told her to read all the books; now though, Mary knew that she wouldn't.

CHAPTER
ELEVEN

Night had fallen and Mary sat in the middle of the room; it didn't really matter to her that the fire didn't burn to keep her warm. She had gotten used to the cold as she'd sat there with her thoughts. Tending to the books had made her feel as if she had a role to play in the village, which in turn made her feel part of it. She'd also realised that because she'd rescued a sorcerer there would be no good luck from the dragons...but the possibility of the opposite remained.

Mary heard feet crunching the glass on the stone floor and looked up in time to see Prater stop suddenly in the doorway; water dripped from his clothing and began to form small puddles on the floor. While his men continued towards the stairs, his head moved around the room – Mary had spent most of the night replacing the books to their rightful homes.

"It's freezing in here," Prater's voice echoed in the room.

Mary's eyes trailed away from Prater and back to her feet that rested against the floor. She reached up and tugged on the light brown shawl that loosely wrapped over her shoulders so that she could feel it against her dress.

"Shouldn't you be with your dragon? You are bound after all, aren't you?"

Mary pulled the sleeve of her dress down to cover her binding mark. "I was not bound to him."

"Not bound to the dragon, okay, let's say for the sake of argument I believe you." Prater paused and continued to look in Mary's direction as she stood up. "Maybe then the second one, if Cecilia is a sorceress but then why would she be angry with you; so maybe you're bound to a sorcerer then?"

"No." Mary turned and walked to another desk; once seated, she trailed her fingers over the swirls and lines of the grain.

Prater faltered in his expression as a few of his men headed upstairs to search Mary's bedchamber. She watched the corridor until it had emptied, and then she turned her attention back to the patterns in the wood on the desktop.

"Neither?"

Mary heard Prater's hard-soled shoes echo across the stone bricks as he approached her. He crouched down beside the desk and moved Mary's hair away from her face.

"Then who are you bound to?" His face moved closer to hers.

"It doesn't matter," Mary whispered. Her eyes twitched every time she heard a noise above; as she listened, something hit the floor with a thud, followed by a crunching sound – the reflection board.

"It does matter, Mary," Prater paused and reached his right hand out to lift Mary's chin so he could look in her eyes. "It matters, Mary, because I need to know if someone is going to come looking for you."

The words sent a shiver down Mary's spine, similar to the type of feeling she got when she walked past the burial yard outside of town. People went there to remember, to grieve, but for Mary it had always been a place for dead things, evil things. Prater held Mary's face, his fingers positioned in the same position that Quinn had held her but it didn't elicit the same feelings inside her.

"No one will come looking for me, Master Prater." She continued to avoid eye contact with him as she dealt with feelings of sadness and defeat. Without her gift of reading she felt lost and without purpose.

"Tell me who he is, Mary…and I'll leave this building as it is now."

"Who?"

"Who you are bound to, Mary?" Prater asked. "It was one of the men you rescued; I don't believe your story about a book-keeper."

Raising her head, Mary said, "He is not a book-keeper, not a dragon, and not a sorcerer. I make mistakes in the same way that you do and have in the past."

"Tell me his name…tell me his name or I will destroy all this."

"Even you wouldn't be so foolish as to try and destroy the books again," Mary replied with a smile; she spoke the words with confidence knowing that the threat couldn't be fulfilled.

Prater sneered. He removed his hand from Mary's face and leaned back on his heels to consider his next question.

"Life could have been so different without dragons and sorcerers. Look at how the magic guides even what we humans do. I mean, you don't welcome any strangers to our village. Trade only occurs if you or one of your men has vetted the poor person, probably to the point of distraction. We live in fear of the other two kingdoms because of the past, because of that magic both the other sides possess." Mary paused watching Prater for a moment. "Do you really believe that all those men you hung were dragons?"

"It is possible."

"Okay, let's say that they were all dragon, huh? What exactly do you think those dragons might have done? You threaten the books but it's not like the night when you were determined to destroy them. Why should you feel the need to kill them if we are abiding by the rules?"

"You know nothing about why I need to protect this village from them! This isn't just about the books Mary, there is so much more to this!" Prater replied clenching his fist. "We all have lost in this village. Not a day goes by that I don't think about that night and what happened to my own father. You've spent ten years in this building with all these books but how much do you really know about people and life, Mary?"

"About the same as you I would think, though perhaps we see things differently. Dragons are not the enemy." Mary paused as she heard footsteps on the stairs.

"We've gone through every room except this one, Master," Delwyn said as he entered the main room.

"No need to search in here, the door is elsewhere – you must have missed something. It will be something small, insignificant, hiding the way. It will be somewhere on this floor..." Prater's head slowly titled to one side as he watched her. "On second thought, tell the men they can leave – you as well, Delwyn – Mary is going to show me where the door is."

"As you order, Master," Delwyn replied and walked back to the passage room. "Men, we're done here for the moment; return to your daily life."

As the men filtered out of the building, Prater stepped forward and watched them leave. He closed the large doors to the room they were in and turned back to Mary.

"Now, where were we? That's right; you were trying to tell me that dragons are not the enemy? Let me tell you about dragons. I was fifteen when I went into the Great Forest with my father to hunt. We came across this man there – a stranger; he told us to be careful to not go deeper into the forest that day. He seemed half-mad, a dishevelled old man with torn clothing and one eye missing – he just had this nasty scar cutting across where it should have been. Father and I kept on hunting. I'd grown up hunting in that forest; we'd never seen anything to fear in there except for our own imaginations. We were following a deer and saw it enter a clearing — a clear shot. Father had his arrow ready to fly when this bloody dragon swooped down. It grabbed that deer in its claws and then looked at us. The sound, Mary, I'd never heard anything like it, louder than a bear and fierce. When I looked to Father, he'd fallen to the ground, his hand over his chest. When I turned back the dragon was gone and I ran blindly back to the village for help."

"Dragons can't kill with sound…"

"No, but people can die of fright! The dragon killed my father. My father and I were close, and the dragon took him away." Prater paced back and forth, his hands calming for a moment before he looked back over at Mary. "As I ran for the village, I came across that man. You know what he did? He smiled at me and nodded, then said: 'They're coming for all humans, boy, and no sorcerer will save you, best remember that.' I never saw him again, but I've ensured that I've protected this village ever since."

"Protected? Is that what you call it? It was your fault we lost over half the village on the night of the burning; your fault – nobody else's."

"I didn't know that would happen. I just wanted to make the dragons feel the same pain I was in." Prater paused and pushed the loose hair away from Mary's face. "If my twin hadn't died after birth then he would have perished too. I don't know, maybe then it would never have happened because he would have been the leader and not me. After that though, I made sure strangers stayed away. You'll never understand it Mary, the dragons in your mind are nothing more than images you've created based on books written by dragons. It's not like they're going to write a book that says 'Hey, dragons are people-killing monsters.'"

"You blame the dragons for taking your father away, yet you've taken away more from others. What if all those men, fourteen you've hung, were just human? Huh? Tell me Prater, who is the real monster then?"

Shaking his head, Prater exhaled. "And what if every single one was really a dragon? Or maybe a sorcerer? One of them was a dragon...that much I am sure of...one of the last two I think...which one was it, Mary?" Prater leaned forward and shook Mary by her shoulders. "Or maybe it was this other mystery man?"

Mary shook her head and moved her eyes to stare past him. She feared he had begun to piece together a theory and subsequent questions that would require answers. Prater sneered and removed his hands. He wandered over to one of the shelves and picked a random book. He returned to Mary with it in his hand. "Maybe the answer to my question is in this book?"

"Maybe it is."

"What's it about?" Prater threw the book so that it landed right in front of Mary with a resounding thud.

That's a good question, Mary thought. She looked at the cover of the book. Lines, curves – she knew they were letters, but which ones she had no idea; frustrated, her eyebrows drew nearer to each other. *Why couldn't the book he chose have had a picture on the cover?*

"Well, Mary, what is this book about?"

Mary looked at it and decided that since he couldn't read either, it wouldn't matter what she said, "It's about crops, how to look after them and everything."

Prater walked back over to her and crouched down. Picking up the book, Prater turned it over in his hand so that the front cover faced upwards. "If it's about crops then why is the title 'A History of Village Buildings'?"

"It's not."

"It is. You see, I know how to read, just like you. Call it my little secret...our little secret now."

Mary glanced up to study Prater's expression, expecting to see something, maybe playfulness or a joke, but his face spoke only of seriousness. Her eyes widened in shock.

"Read, but..."

"No questions on that matter at the moment. What I don't understand is that since you know how to read, why lie about what this book is about?"

Shrugging her shoulders, Mary replied, "Didn't think it mattered."

"Well, Mary, it does matter. Now that you know my secret, I want to know yours."

Mary turned her face further away from Prater's even though she knew it would accomplish nothing. "It's not just my secret, so I can't tell it."

"Then tell me where the tunnel is." He leaned close with an insincere smile plastered on his face.

Mary wondered how he could know about the tunnel; her fingers gripped the fabric of her skirt. "What tunnel, Master?"

"The one that leads from the book building to the cell." Mary gulped and bit her lip. She tapped her foot against the floor, grateful it made no noise.

"There's a tunnel?" Mary knew the awkward change in pitch gave her away. Prater reached out, touched Mary's shoulder and leant back on his heels, just slightly.

"You know there's tunnel, Mary. Delwyn and I just spent the better part of a few hours going over every inch of that cell. We found it, the deeper indentation around a set of bricks. I couldn't get the door to open though so I suspect that it can only be done from one side – the other side, where the tunnel is."

"That's an interesting story."

"Mary, here's what I think. The last two men vanished from that cell, and I believe it was you who let them free." Mary cast her eyes down since Prater's touch prevented her from turning her body further away. "You thought them to be special, didn't you, Mary? Perhaps it was something you read?"

"I have read a lot of things in a lot of books, Master."

"You haven't answered my question, Mary."

"I don't know about a tunnel or how those men vanished from the cell."

"But you told me that the first of the two was *special* Mary, you said you had read something, and we should treat him right."

"I did read something, but it did not say that he would vanish from the cell…"

"You mean be assisted in an escape…"

"I don't…"

"I know, Mary, you don't know anything about it, right?" Prater pursed his lips.

Mary tried to continue focusing away from him but when Prater shifted his head to the side her gaze returned to his face. She felt his hand as it moved from her cheek and down to her chin, raising Mary's face up he forced her to look into his eyes.

"I can smash that stone door in that is in the cell and follow it Mary, make no mistake that I will do that if necessary."

She didn't want that. Yansa had entrusted the knowledge of the tunnels to her. Her heart fell knowing she had likely failed in keeping that a secret already. Thoughts raced through her mind and the sorceress' face flashed in her mind. "Perhaps it was that woman who freed the men…"

"Do you think me simple, Mary? Do you think that I can be so easily fooled?" Prater smiled at his own statement. "You're not good at lying, Mary – just tell me the truth."

"I don't know what you're talking about."

Prater nodded. "Guess you'll just have to spend some time in the cell, after all. I doubt anyone will come to rescue you – and if they do, I'll be waiting."

"You can't be serious. You're saying you're going to lock me up until you get your dragon?" Mary finally turned to look Prater directly in the eyes, resolute to know what her future had in store.

The bad luck has started, Mary thought, she blamed herself for binding to a mere mortal and then stupidly rescuing a sorcerer. *The dragons are not happy with what I did.*

"We're going to find the way into the cell from here. I doubt that you can get out of the cell from inside it – no, you would need someone to open it. I will allow the men time to rest and go about their daily business, but make no mistake, Mary – we will find that tunnel. Until you give up the tunnel, or your dragon, you can consider the cell your new home. All you have to do is give him up, a name, place...or better yet you could just call him to you. I've read they come when called...especially since you're bound."

"I am not bound to a dragon so no one would come if I called. I've told you already that I'm bound to a mere mortal. There is nothing else that you need to know about that!" Mary spat back, as angry with herself as Prater.

"I could have made you happy, Mary, but I guess we're never going to know." He stood up and then grabbed Mary's arm, pulling her to her feet. "I'm sure you'll find the cell comfortable. I will keep tearing apart this building until not one book is left on any of the shelves."

Mary tried to push him away, to free herself from his grip. As she pushed against him, she looked up to see Delwyn standing in the doorway.

"Master, do you think that's necessary?"

Prater's head whipped around and glowered at Delwyn, "Who is the leader of this village?"

For a moment Mary wondered if Delwyn might help but then saw him look away. The other men could be heard descending the stairs and Prater nodded towards the narrow book room. With a nod of his head Mary watched as Delwyn avoided looking at her and directed the men away from them.

Tightening his grip, Prater dragged Mary out through the opening of the book building and across the dark muddy way to the cell. Prater closed the gold door on Mary, leaving her in total darkness.

In her solitude, Mary curled her knees up to meet her chin. Burying her face between them, she allowed, at last, all the tears to fall freely from her eyes.

CHAPTER
TWELVE

Back at home, Quinn sat down in the seat beside the fire, stretched out his legs, and sighed. His eyes were heavy, and he struggled to keep them open; it had been a long day – all things considered. He felt angry and annoyed at his sister's behaviour, but he considered that it wasn't anything new. All his life he had followed the rules and he knew he had started to creep close to breaking the Golden Law but part of him wanted to justify it away.

But then again, he seethed in own defence, *I didn't do anything; didn't get the chance to be more truthful. For a moment there in that village with Mary, that could have been something more, but I'll never know thanks to my reckless sister.*

Walking into his kitchen, he grabbed a glass and looked around for a bucket of water. He'd grown accustomed to doing things manually and smiled. Waving his hand, the glass filled with water; he watched it for a moment as the water settled.

Quinn had always been determined to ensure Cecilia didn't win at the game she played; if he let her beat him on this, then there would be no stopping her. As Quinn's thoughts churned, Cashel entered the room slowly, as old men tend to take their time and Cashel was no exception.

"You've been gone sometime," Cashel commented as he took relief in the wicker chair beside Quinn.

"Concerned?"

"Of course I was concerned. Did you find Michael?"

Quinn hung his head and shook it, "No, I didn't find Michael."

"Then you're going to need your rest. Cecilia will not rest until they are bound."

"She has a major obstacle to overcome then," Quinn replied.

Cashel looked over at Quinn who stared at the flickering flames, thinking of Mary. Since Quinn left Mary behind, he'd felt guilty; he kept thinking that he should go back...*but to do what?* He had no plan...his life had been consumed with stopping his sister for so long that he had had no time to think about anything else, to make any other plans.

"What do you mean?"

"Michael is bound already to another."

Cashel smiled with surprise and relief. "That is very good news; very good news indeed. Quinn, for the first time in months, I can sit back and relax. I might even get a decent night's sleep!"

"Not so good news for the girl," Quinn mumbled.

"Speak up, Quinn, if you have something to say."

Quinn continued to stare at the fire and kicked off his boots. "I said it's not so great for the girl he got bound to."

"Why ever not? If Michael has finally come to his senses and seen through your sister and bound to another – well, that all seems like a perfect ending to this entire dilemma. Plus, it will release you from your task and you can…"

"He left her behind in the village," the words blurted out. Quinn held his head with his hands and closed his eyes.

"And you know this for a fact, do you?" Cashel inquired, looking at his apprentice to see his reaction.

"She was in the village, she had the binding mark, and he was nowhere to be found. Yes, I would say he abandoned her," Quinn's replied, frustrated at having to justify his own assessment of the situation to his mentor.

"Nothing else? Have you seen your sister?"

"She made an appearance; she's a little *upset* by the situation."

"No matter, Quinn; your sister can't kill her, and the binding will remain until one of them dies, so as far as I can tell, Cecilia will need to choose a new target and start again if she is so determined in her quest."

Quinn scoffed and turned to his mentor. "So, you're saying that the girl's future is of no consequence to us? Are you really so naïve to think that Cecilia is going to spend another ten years searching for a man whose bloodline is free of both dragon and sorcerer blood?"

"Quinn, what has gotten into you?" Quinn broke the eye contact first and his mentor sat back in his chair glaring. "What happened?"

"Nothing happened."

"Something happened," Cashel paused before continuing, "You know, I'm old, but I'm not stupid. Something has happened, I can see the change as clear as day in your behaviour. Something happened which has changed you and I want to know what."

Quinn watched the flames. *So much has changed. I've spent ten years of my life doing what the Sorcery Council assigned to me and because of that almost got hung. No matter her reasons, Mary saved my life.*

"What about me, Cashel? I had no choice but to spend my time tracking Cecilia all over the place to satisfy the Sorcery Council, but what about me? When do I get to stop and have a life?"

"When the job is done, which now it is. I know you had to take on a lot of responsibility young. You've dedicated a lot of time to this, and perhaps that's been at the expense of..."

"Of having a life."

"Now that sounds like Cecilia."

Quinn shook his head. "Maybe Cecilia is right about that. I have nothing Cashel; you've had a long life, but I feel like I'm old and I'm not. I'd like to catch up with friends, I'd like to..."

"To what? What happened Quinn?"

Quinn pushed up his sleeve, faint red marks still circled around his wrists. Cashel reached out and grabbed his arm.

"Gold?"

"I didn't realise how quickly it took effect."

"But you're okay now?"

Quinn's head shook back and forth. *No, I'm not okay.*

"I'm tired."

"What makes you tired? What happened this time, Quinn?"

"I'll tell you tomorrow."

Quinn abruptly stood up and walked away from Cashel, knowing full well how disrespectful it appeared; he trudged up the wooden steps and into his bedroom, closing the wooden door on the world and collapsing on his bed.

# CHAPTER THIRTEEN

"It doesn't have to be this way, Mary," Prater said, kneeling in the light that streamed from the outside and through the open cell door.

Mary purposely kept her head lowered, partly because she didn't want to look at Prater and partly because the light hurt her eyes. Mary had been in the cell for many days and felt weak. Every day, Prater pestered her about dragons and sorcerers, and every day Mary said nothing. She had curled herself into the corner near the tunnel exit in the wall – from the little conversation that had drifted into the cell she knew that Prater had not been back into the book building since he had imprisoned her – consequently he had not found the tunnel entrance yet either.

"Mary, please." Prater squatted not far away from her, but he was merely a shape silhouetted by the light. "At least eat something. You're no use to me dead."

"I'm no use to you alive either," Mary replied, the first time she had spoken a word since he had thrown her in the cell. Many times, in the darkness of the cell, she had wished that she had gone with Michael, not parted ways, but if wishes were real she would be a very different person.

"Where can I find the dragon? Which one was the dragon?" She let her head fall against the stone wall and rolled her eyes.

"Neither was probably a dragon. I don't know. How many times do I have to keep telling you the same thing? You see, Master Prater, if one of them had been a dragon and I had helped him escape, that would mean that I had helped one. If all that were true then according to the information I've read about them, I should be experiencing good luck as a reward. Does it look like I'm blessed with luck?"

Prater hung his head before he pushed his fallen hair back away from his face. "Tell me the name of the sorceress."

Mary knew the answer to that one and wondered whether it would be of any harm to tell

Prater. She conceded to herself that it would not. "Her name is Cecilia."

Prater smiled at the useful information. "Finally, something I can work with." He stood and held out his hand. "Come on, Mary, we'll see about finding you some more comfortable surroundings. I really don't like to see you in here, despite what you might be thinking."

Mary looked over at him and asked, "What are you going to do with me?"

"I haven't decided yet."

"Are you going to hang me like the others?"

Prater leaned back against the wall, taking a moment to look in the direction of her freedom.

"Even I could not convince this village that you were worthy of that honour." He walked over and attempted to pull Mary to her feet. "I will have to think about what to do with you. I knew you'd tell me something, sooner or later. I have a room prepared for you; your things are already there. What is wrong with you?"

Weak from having refused to eat or drink and feeling broken, Mary found that she had no energy to stand even if she wanted to. Unexpectedly, Prater bent down and lifted Mary up into his arms. The sunlight assaulted her face as Prater walked outside, and she shielded her eyes from the light with her arm. Though she couldn't see much, she knew the village well enough to know they were heading to Prater's home.

The coolness of being inside the house and shielded from the sun should have made Mary feel relief. Instead, with her arm lowered, her eyes darted around the interior as Prater walked through an entrance area and down a short passage that met another door. She felt grateful to be out of the cell but the thought of living under the same roof as Prater made her fingers dig into his shoulder.

Inside the room, Prater placed Mary into a chair to the right of the fireplace. Curiously her eyes scanned the room, taking in what she could see. She had often wondered what the house looked like inside and imagined it with elaborate carvings on the wood panelling and marble floors. Instead she found it to be quite simple.

Her eyes fell on two paintings that hung on the stone chimney. Mary couldn't remember Prater's father at all, and his mother had died when he'd been born according to Yansa. With their faces staring out from the canvases Mary felt uncomfortable thinking how Prater had made decisions to protect people after losing those closest to him. A part of her could understand his actions even though the rest of her said his actions were still wrong. After staring at the paintings for a short time, Mary closed her eyes and tried to remember her own parents and sister, but no images materialised in her mind.

Saddened, Mary focused on scrutinising the room further. A vase on the table to the side of the fireplace filled an otherwise bare corner, an oak sideboard to Mary's right. Adjusting her position on the chair, Mary attempted to look farther behind her but found Prater instead, leaning casually against the doorframe watching her study his room. Mary sunk back into the chair embarrassed at her own inquisitiveness.

"I've ran a bath for you, in your room." Prater's voice spoke low, soft, but to Mary it still sounded as if it were an order, so she stood up from the chair. Mary raised her gaze to look at Prater - he half-smiled in return before turning and leading Mary to her new room.

The few clothes Mary had were hung up neatly over a wooden pole. Her hairbrush and a couple of leather ties she used to secure her hair beneath her snood lay on a small wooden table. Mary glanced over everything and then looked at the bath. The hot water tempted her as she watched the steam rise from the surface, especially after the time in the cell. She decided to take advantage of the situation.

Feeling human again after bathing, Mary felt comforted wearing fresh, clean clothes again. As she brushed her hair, she looked at her belongings that sat on the table next to the bed.

"Where did you come from?" she said quietly to herself and picked up a small stone. It certainly hadn't been one of her belongings. Turning it over in her hand she studied the little blue and green stone; its swirls reminded Mary of the patterns in the sky which appeared from time to time – though never green – yet there was a familiarity about the stone that certainly did remind Mary of something, or perhaps it was someone...

A knock on her door and Mary stowed the stone in the pocket of her dress, holding it firmly with her left hand for reassurance.

"Yes?"

"May I come in, Mary?" She would have liked to reply in the negative, but she didn't want to end up back in the cell.

"Yes."

"No need to hide the binding mark, Mary. I already know." Mary grasped the stone once more before letting it rest in the pocket of its own accord and withdrew her hand.

"What would you like?"

"I want to know more about this Cecilia…she seemed to know a lot about you."

"I've told you all I know," Mary replied with the partial truth – she didn't want to tell him about Quinn.

"Where is this Cecilia from?"

"I don't know."

"She said she was your sister by binding…"

"She was lying…"

"Then you know she has a brother. Who was he?"

Mary looked away from Prater and bit her lip.

"Mary?" Prater eyed Mary carefully.

"Are you bound to her brother?"

"No, I am not bound to her brother."

"So, you admit that she has a brother?" Mary quickly looked up, caught out.

Prater smiled at his success. "He was the second one, I think. Yes, yes, your reaction gives you away."

Prater took a step towards Mary; she backed up closer to the pillow on the bed and continued to avoid eye contact.

"Why protect a sorcerer, Mary? Sorcerers live their lives separate from humans. They care nothing for us, that's something they stopped doing a long time ago."

"I'm not protecting anyone."

"Then tell me who he is."

"I don't know, he said he was looking for his brother Jack, that's all I know."

Prater stepped back and Mary saw his fingers tap against his leg: one, two three. She anticipated a question but instead Prater threw a bag onto the bed beside her. Cautiously, she opened it and found a fresh bread roll – she knew them well, as the woman always included one in her food box. She ripped a small piece off and chewed it well, relishing the taste. It didn't take long for the roll to be gone.

"Are you ready to show me where the entrance is Mary?"

Mary didn't respond.

"Come on."

Outside in the fresh air, Mary noticed the villagers just continued on with whatever they were doing – there were a few glances in her direction, but each person glanced away from Mary when she caught their eye.

Mary looked twice when she saw the door to the book building had been replaced with an identical one. She hardly had time to look it over as Prater pulled her through the doorway and inside the building. Once inside he paused to bolt the door. They were locked in.

"Thought you would like that. Having the door fixed." An awkward silence descended over the pair, standing in the passage room. "Where is the entrance, Mary?"

"Why does it matter?" Mary quietly asked as her fingers fidgeted with the fabric of her dress.

"Secrets do no one any good, Mary. I want you to trust me." Prater moved to stand in front of her.

"Why?"

"Because I want you, Mary. You must know that by now." Mary's fingers involuntarily made a fist as they clutched the fabric. Prater's hand reached up and he ran his fingers through her loose hair. She felt warmth spreading across her cheeks despite herself. He leaned in closer and Mary stepped back – only to find the wall.

"Mary."

Risking a glimpse at Prater's face, Mary thought he seemed genuine, but she suspected that control, knowledge, and power were the motivation, not feelings. He just wanted to know about the tunnel. Prater had noticed the spared glance and moved closer again.

"I am already bound, Master Prater." Prater's free hand covered her left that still gripped the fabric of her dress tightly.

"But what if you weren't, Mary?"

Mary's feet shifted; she didn't like this game he was playing at all.

"The entrance is through the narrow book room."

Prater paused, his thumb gently stroking Mary's cheek a couple of times before he stepped back. His right hand still holding onto her left, he used that connection to lead her to the narrow room
.

After he looked around the room, he turned to Mary and asked, "Where's the entrance exactly?"

Shaking Prater's hand free, she stepped up onto the bottom shelf and pushed the disarray of books that remained on the shelf to the side. She stood on her tippy-toes and reached back to the lever that barely protruded from the back of the bookcase.

Prater smiled as he watched the bookcase move. Mary wiped her dusty hand on her apron, and reached in to touch the stone, holding it tightly as she watched Prater step through the doorway, and down the steps before returning, no doubt, for a torch.

CHAPTER FOURTEEN

Mary stirred in her bed; sleep would not come, and she had grown tired of trying to convince it otherwise. Throwing the blankets to the side, she lit a candle and sat still, listening for any sound. She couldn't hear any obvious noises and glanced at the window and saw the night sky.

Swinging her legs beside the bed, her feet her felt the soft mat below her feet. Her eyes travelled to her shoes, but she shook her head. The candle's light just reached the bottom part of the door and she tapped the fingers on her free hand.

Oh, what does it matter if I have a look around. If he's asleep he'll never know. She paused halfway to the door at that thought. *If he is awake, I'll just say I need...a glass of water.* Mary turned to see that a glass sat on her bedside table.

With the candle on the floor, she went to the window and pushed it up; a breeze whipped in and the flame dwindled but stayed alight. Grabbing the glass, she poured the water outside before returning it to the table.

Candle back in her hand, Mary double checked she'd closed the window and took small steps towards the door. Slowly she turned the handle and the door opened without a peep. Her head poked into the hallway and she saw only darkness except for a light glowing under the door of the living room where she had sat before.

She made her way toward the beckoning light; her bare feet made no sound on the floorboards. As a barrier the door did its job, but Mary smiled at seeing the keyhole. Bending down she squinted and peered through the tiny hole to see that the candles burned brightly within the room. She moved away to extinguish her own flame before returning to spy on her captor.

Prater watched the flames dancing on the logs. She saw that he sat in his father's large wooden armchair to the side of the fireplace – she'd often seen the chair on the porch when she'd walked past with her mother to collect water from the well. He seemed deep in thought as his elbows rested on the arms and his fingers formed a peak on his lips. She suspected his thoughts would be about the tunnel, no longer secret. She knew he'd want to fully explore each and every part of the labyrinth.

"You sit so silently," the feminine voice broke the crackling of the fire as a delicate hand rested on Prater's shoulder. Mary saw him start slightly at the intrusion, and her heart pounded in her chest at the sight of Quinn's sister. Prater though, once he leaned back, regained his composed expression.

"This is the last place I thought to see you."

Cecilia's cynical laughter followed, and she moved towards the fireplace. Her eyes momentarily watched the flames before she turned back to look at Prater.

"Cecilia, I presume."

Her lips flinched slightly "I am Cecilia, and yes, I suppose it is a rather unusual place for me to be, but you see, that useless little book-keeper has left me in a little predicament. Plus, your men have been asking a lot of questions in the neighbouring towns which is making my life unpleasant. I thought perhaps we could come to an...an arrangement."

"I would rather be rid of you. Sorcerers are no more welcome in this village than dragons."

"Now, now, I came here to play nicely."

"How would I be able to assist you? What has Mary done exactly?"

"Mary has become bound to a man. A man that I was to be bound to."

"So, choose a new man; I am not bound."

Cecilia laughed and looked around the room dismissively.

"I chose that man for a reason; it must be him. Michael possesses a rare quality that is difficult and rather time consuming to discover. I don't have the patience to waste another ten years finding a suitable replacement."

"So, is this man a sorcerer, too? Or perhaps he is a dragon?" Prater asked, fishing for information. Mary, too, felt curious about Michael; he had seemed like a regular human by the time they parted.

"Nothing of the sort, he is just a mere mortal – much like yourself."

"A mortal?" Prater contemplated the words before looking back at the sorceress. "So, Mary told the truth about the binding to me. I'm surprised to hear that."

"I can't help you with any of that; all I know is that I'm in a bind of my own due to that girl's actions."

"Does this man have a name?"

"Of course he has a name, but it is not something you need to know." Cecilia continued to stand, her presence demanding attention, and yet she stood calmly.

Prater pursed his lips in frustration, narrowed his eyes on Cecilia, and asked cautiously, "What is it that you think I can do?"

"I need that binding broken, but a little oath I took at The Academy prevents me from doing so. After all, I like having power, magic, and I am not about to give that up without a hell of a fight."

"I don't know how to break a binding – except if one of them dies."

Cecilia raised her eyebrows, smiled at Prater, and laughed.

"I'm not going to kill Mary, if you were hoping for that. It seems to me that you have a lot to lose if you don't break the binding – I have a lot of power here in the village to lose and I won't compromise that either."

Mary breathed relief that Prater drew a line at some things. She shifted her feet, as one had begun to feel numb, but regretted the pins and needles that replaced it. Grimacing, she moved her head to try and gain a different view of the conversation.

Cecilia took a step closer to Prater and leaned forward so that their eyes were level. "You really are a prince, aren't you? Luckily for you, I am not allowed to kill Mary, and having someone else do the killing is also against Academy rules, unfortunately. There are those that say the dragons can break a binding."

"So, what does that have to do with me?"

"Books, Prater, it will be in the books." Cecilia straightened herself upright and stepped back towards the fireplace, maintaining eye contact all the while. "The dragons record everything; in one of those books there will be a way to break the binding. I want you to find it."

"You want me to find one book in that book building?"

"I know you can read – there is no point in playing coy with me."

"I guess I shouldn't dare ask how you know."

Mary's curiosity about how Cecilia knew he could read had been piqued as well but supposed she may have bluffed it. Prater's expression would have been enough to confirm it anyway as he interlocked his fingers together, rested them casually against his stomach, and sunk a little deeper into the chair.

"And what would I get out of all this?"

"Why that meddling book-keeper would be free of her binding of course."

Mary glanced down at the binding mark, and then back to Prater in time to see a contemptuous smile appear on his face.

"I need more than just Mary free of a binding – after all, look at what you would be gaining should I be successful."

Cecilia growled, and placed her hands on her hips. "What is it that you want?"

"Let me think on it."

"I did not come here to leave empty-handed; give me an answer."

"Something of this magnitude requires thought and consideration – you are free to stay and wait, but I have no idea how long it will be before I make my decision."

Cecilia sighed. The neutral expression she'd maintained so far faded as her eyebrows knitted together and her lips pursed.

"I would have thought that a man with your power would be more decisive."

Prater unlocked his fingers, and gestured his hands outwards, nonchalantly.

"Very well. I will return in one week, no earlier and no later – have your answer ready or I might just decide to cease playing nicely." Cecilia raised her hands and vanished in a spray of blue light.

Prater refolded his hands and glanced around the room.

"Well, that was unexpected. I could just ignore her, or then again, I could ask for wealth, but there isn't much use for that here – same can be said for wanting property. No, if I am to help her, I need to have some benefit for myself. "

Prater stood suddenly, and Mary leaned back too fast and fell against the wall. She hurriedly stood, bolted for her room, and slid under the blankets. Her heart thudded as she tried to keep her eyes relaxed, her body still, and her breathing shallow. Maintaining all that would have been easier without hearing Prater's steady stride coming closer to the door. The footsteps ceased, and she tried swallowing despite her mouth being dry.

"Get a grip," he muttered before the door swung open and a moment later closed again, taking the light that had glowed with it.

Mary opened one eye and then the other. She breathed out slowly when she saw that no one else occupied the room. Shifting to a more comfortable position, she snuggled down beneath the blanket; thoughts of what to do about Cecilia's plan kept her awake.

CHAPTER
FIFTEEN

"Mary, where are you going?"

Her breath ricocheted off the door and she grimaced at how close she'd come.

"I thought that...I thought the books should go back on the shelves."

Prater stood in the doorway to the living room, and she was annoyed that her plan had been foiled. She had hoped to locate the book and conceal it somewhere before he'd realised she'd left, thinking it seemed the obvious one to have the information he wanted. Being bound to Michael seemed infinitely better than having it broken and facing the alternative in front of her.

"Good idea, Mary, wouldn't want to upset the dragons, now would we? I'll come too."

As Mary and Prater walked towards the book building, she glanced around at her home village but found no one willing to make eye contact, everyday tasks suddenly much more involved than they once were. She spared a glance at Prater but found him focused ahead.

For a time, Prater and Mary were amongst the books in silence. Mary set about piling up the books and shelving them, her eyes scanning each similar cover for the dragon engraving. She had thought of trying to hide it amongst a larger pile, or maybe towards the top of the shelves, but knew that any of those actions were more likely to draw Prater's attention than divert it.

"Why not bring a few back to the house?"

Mary looked up at Prater, surprised at the offer. "Before I would have but now there's no point."

"How so? Come on, most the time you spend with these books, surely you enjoy them a little."

"I used to but that was before."

"Before what?"

"Before I could read and now I can't. Consequences abound it would seem for everything I try to do."

"People don't just forget a skill like reading. It would be like me forgetting how to ride a horse - after a while it becomes second nature. Why would you pretend you can't read?" She looked over at him as he held a book in his own hand.

I wish I could believe that I was just pretending the lines meant nothing. She ran her finger over the embossed bridge on the cover of the book she held.

"Is it easier if I just say that books aren't important to me anymore? Would that be easier for you to accept?" Mary replied and continued to put the book on top of her pile. Lifting the stack, she headed for the nearest shelves and began offloading them.

"Okay, I'll humour you. You suddenly can't read because of whatever reason. Why put them back on the shelves then? Let's forget that dragon excuse - there are hundreds of book buildings across the kingdom that have become dusty and the dragons haven't sought revenge that we've heard. Why not just ignore all this and walk away from it?"

"It gives me something to do."

"We have so little in our lives, it's almost a little pathetic. Perhaps you can help me then." She glanced over at him as he sat down at one of the desks – more specifically the one that had once been her favourite. "I'm after a book, a very specific book – perhaps one that Yansa didn't want you to read."

"There are lots of books I haven't read…"

"But how many didn't Yansa want you to read?"

Just the one, Mary thought to herself, *well, just the one I know of.*

"I don't know about all the books, Master." Mary grabbed a red leather-bound book, the final in the stack she'd moved, and placed it on the lowest of shelves trying to ignore Prater's unyielding gaze.

"What about *the* book?"

"*The* book?"

"The one you read; the book that prompted you to rescue those men from the cell. Tell me, Mary, which book persuaded you to take such drastic action?"

"A brown-covered one," Mary replied. She hadn't lied but felt pleased with her answer – the book did have a brown cover and with such a generic title she could hardly point him in the right direction.

"You're going to need to be a bit more specific, Mary."

Mary looked at the cover of the book in her hand and while she couldn't read the title, she knew that the book contained information about flowers due to the dragon-rose flower embossed into the leather cover.

"It has a dragon on the cover." *Just like a hundred other books here do.*

Mary couldn't help but smile as she watched Prater move off to a pile of books with conviction. She took pleasure knowing he would find a large collection of brown books with dragons on them. If the books hadn't been tossed to the floor in such a haphazard way, she may have considered offering assistance, but the distance would be easier if she found the book first.

With Prater busy in his own book quest, Mary relaxed at the distance that now separated them. Adjusting her kneeling position, a portion of her apron clicked against the stone floor – unnoticed by Prater who failed miserably at conducting a search quietly.

Reaching into the pocket of her apron, Mary retrieved the little blue and green stone. Another glance in Prater's direction saw that he was occupied by his task, and Mary's shoulders slackened as she stared at the stone. Again, as she focused on the swirls that almost appeared to be moving, she felt a sense of familiarity about the stone...the longer she stared, the stronger the feeling grew. The smoothness of the stone, quiet and unassuming...the swirls of blue and green; a hint of a smile appeared on Mary's face. Quinn. The colours of the stone reminded her of the sorcerer's eyes – eyes that she had foolishly thought had belonged to a dragon.

A loud thud from behind startled Mary and the stone dropped from her fingers and landed soundlessly on the fabric of her dress. Prater cursed a book that he had dropped directly on his foot, attempting to shift it away with his other; Mary knew that one well, as she'd often struggled to lift the book herself. As much as she tried to suppress the smile on her face, she felt it spread in amusement. Prater looked up and their eyes met for a moment before Mary turned back to her own pile of books. Out of sight, Mary recovered the stone from the folds of her dress's fabric and returned it to the safety of the apron pocket.

****

As Mary turned over in the bed, she could hear Prater's pacing footsteps echoing through the house. She hadn't planned on leaving the bed but when the pacing ceased, she made her way to the room down the corridor.

He had paused near one of the paintings of his parents, his face concentrating on their faces that stared out blankly. The flash of light from the corner didn't draw his attention but Mary recognised it immediately.

"Prater."

"Don't you ever use the front door?" Prater turned to face her and his foot slipped on the wood. He reached out his hand steady himself. Mary smiled and stifled the urge to laugh at the way Prater attempted to cover the undignified movement.

"Doors are such useless objects; I mean, what exactly do they keep out?" Cecilia waited as Prater pulled both the chairs closer to the fireplace. He motioned with his hand towards one and sat down in the other. "Have you made up your mind then?"

The room fell silent as Prater watched the flames before taking another look at his parents. Mary could see Cecilia's fingers as they tapped rapidly on the arm of the chair, at odds with the calmness of her face.

"I have made up my mind."

"And…come on….I don't have all night."

"You're not the patient type, are you?"

"I planned for ten years and had to be extremely patient during that time; that was all I had in me."

"I will help you to find the spell, but I have a price."

"Riches?"

Prater's shook his head. "No, riches enough I have. I want you to make me younger and to encourage Mary to have feelings for me."

"I must say Prater your choice amuses and surprises me. I can make you younger – that is easy enough to do, but I can't make Mary have feelings for you. Free will is a pain, isn't it?"

"Thankfully," Mary murmured and rubbed her arms against the sudden chill that had swept over her.

"Ah," Prater leaned towards the fire, his forehead creased and his jaw set. "I had thought you powerful enough for anything."

Cecilia laughed lightly. "Once I am bound then maybe I will have that sort of power but for the moment I am unable." Turning her head away from the fire, Cecilia watched as Prater leaned back into his chair. "Surely you don't hold real feelings for Mary, so why should you care if she feels anything for you?"

Mary leaned forward, curious to hear the reply. Prater had made his interest in her known for a while but with so few young women in Tiani since the burning, she wondered if it were more an evitable choice for Prater.

Prater looked over at Cecilia. "Small village, it is better to have someone willing to bind to you rather than forced."

"Then I suggest you use the old-fashioned way to get her to like you," Cecilia paused, "It worked well enough for me."

"I believe women possess far more subtle charms for that purpose compared to most men."

"If you want to secure something, I believe it is worth learning new skills."

"Perhaps then it is because I have tried that already. Perhaps before all this Mary might have agreed but since the binding there is something different about her."

"With the binding broken then you shall have all the time in the world."

Cecilia stood up from the chair and raised her arms to leave.

"Wait."

Cecilia's arms remained where they were.

"How will I let you know that I have found the book?"

"Just read the spell and I will know you have done it." She vanished with a wave of her hand. Mary sat back for a moment, wondering if the book that might break the binding could possibly be in other book buildings. Yansa had told her that not all contained the same books, but she didn't think dragons were stupid enough to not have multiple copies in existence.

If I could get out of here, find someone who could read, maybe I could break the binding myself. She liked the sound of not being in debt to anyone.

"Huh, perhaps I should have asked her exactly how long I would need to wait until she fulfils her promise. Damn, I should have been more explicit with my terms for that agreement," Prater muttered as he grabbed the poker and stirred up the wood; the fire increased and he sat back, his fingers tapping on the arm of the chair.

CHAPTER SIXTEEN

Alone in the book building, Mary enjoyed the moment of solitude. She knew it wouldn't be long before Prater would return, having left when a rider had thundered into Tiani. The books she'd found so far hadn't resembled anything she'd expect to find dragon spells in; it frustrated her knowing she'd over seen one book like the one that had led to the mess she was in.

"Mary," Quinn whispered, and she flinched, moving away from his voice as she turned. "Mary, stop with that."

"I didn't hear you come in."

"I've been here a while, just keeping myself invisible from view. Come on, Prater is busy outside speaking to a messenger. Stop that and come with me."

"And where would we go?"

"I've got a plan, really I have, but now's not the time to talk about it."

Mary looked at Quinn crouched beside her; his blue-green eyes looked back. His hand reached out and gently pushed the book in her hands to the floor, but she didn't let go of it. Quinn's right hand passed in front of his body in a sweeping motion and the books simultaneously rose from the ground. Mary leaned back and watched as the book in her hand wriggled free from her hold and moved into its place on the shelf; all the other books that remained on the floor followed – including all the brown ones Prater had diligently kept separate from the rest.

"Mary, now."

Mary's eyes alternated between the books, the floor, and Quinn. She had hoped he would return but never thought he would. With Quinn so near she felt more alive and safer, her eyes moved away from him and to the window.

Standing up she could see Prater through the window, giving something to the messenger on the horse. She had to make a decision. The book building had been her home, but she had been prepared to leave it all behind for Michael had he been a dragon. If she chose to return one day, she knew that the books would still be there waiting.

"You called me to come back; I won't abandon you again. I promise you that." Mary moved her gaze back to him, wondering what he meant; she hadn't talked to him since she had ordered him to leave. She nodded, half-smiled, and reached out her hand. "You're coming with me?"

Quinn returned the smile and took her hand in his. She felt the warmth of his hand holding hers and her heart fluttered at the feeling spreading throughout her body. With his free hand, Quinn waved and they disappeared from the room in a sparkling cascade of blue-green light.

****

Quinn lay Mary down on the bed in one of the spare bedrooms in his house. He paused looking at her for a moment before standing and leaving the room, being careful to shut the door without making any noise. She was asleep and he wondered if the sudden movement through the sky to home had made her drowsy.

Walking down the narrow wooden staircase, Quinn saw the fire already burning brightly. Cashel sat in the old wicker chair nearby with his eyes closed. Quinn tried not to look at Cashel in case guilt betrayed him.

Quietly, Quinn sat down in the free chair not far from Cashel. Quinn allowed himself to relax and finally feel comfortable with the path he had chosen to take; he closed his own eyes and tried to put the past few weeks behind him.

"You seem to be in a better mood than you have been," Cashel's words floated to Quinn, and he opened his left eye to see Cashel awake and waiting for a response.

"Yeah, well I made a decision today and I feel good about it."

"About your sister? With her plan in tatters, you will have some breathing space; perhaps you might be able to convince her to forget her foolish plan altogether."

"No, not about Cecilia; she'll choose her own path without listening to anything I have to say."

"Are you going to tell me then?"

Quinn refocused his attention on the fire for a moment. He'd never lied to him before, never concealed anything either. Still, he knew it would be inevitable that Cashel would find out about her.

"I brought the girl here. Mary."

"Why did you bring the girl here? It makes you a target to Cecilia."

"I couldn't just leave her there; she was in danger." Quinn turned in his seat to better face Cashel; the older man had been his mentor for many years, and he felt closer to him than he had his own father. Watching Cashel, he wondered if his mentor could understand his reasoning behind the decision.

"Danger? That wasn't why you couldn't leave her behind. That wasn't why you have been out of spirit since you returned, and it certainly wasn't why you suddenly up and left." Cashel shakily rose from his chair with the aid of his walking stick and stood closer to the fire. "You know the rules Quinn – we live our lives by those rules."

"So, I should just ignore my own feelings? Put aside what I want because of what I am?" Angrily, Quinn stood and moved away from the fire in pure frustration.

"Quinn, you were preventing your sister from crossing the same line – it doesn't matter if you have feelings for the mortal or not – you're a sorcerer, she's a mortal! It doesn't matter if she is mixed blood or pure blood. Nothing matters when it comes to that law. You must abide by the treaty that is in place."

"That's also beside the point, Cashel. How could I just leave her behind? She saved my life!" Quinn stood up and joined him in front of the fire.

His hand reached out to hold the mantel as he leaned in closer to the flames. "Cashel..."

"You owe her nothing! She is nothing but an inferior mortal, and now she is one who your sister has placed a spell on."

Cashel turned away from the fire and shuffled back to the chair. Quinn felt frustrated at his mentor knowing so much yet having told him nothing.

"If I had left her there any longer...well, I hate to think what would have happened to her. That village leader might even have killed her. What then, Cashel? If Mary died, then Cecilia would be back on track with her plan in an instant. At least while she is here, she is safe and alive, so Cecilia will be unable to be bound to Michael."

Cashel mumbled something to himself before exhaling slowly, "You are meant to be great, Quinn – you have so much untapped power, maybe even enough to reach the heights of the Council one day – you can't throw it all away by breaking the rules. Another war can't break out because of your *feelings.*"

Quinn turned to look directly as Cashel, "But if Cecilia is bound to Michael the war will happen anyway."

Cashel raised his right hand and pointed an aged finger at his apprentice. "Then you need to keep your emotions in check, keep her safe, but don't fall for her and don't, I mean don't, break the spell that your sister has over her." Quinn turned his back. "Quinn, you must remove your emotions from this matter! You know what I am saying is what you need to do."

Quinn closed his eyes, unwilling to admit aloud that he knew how true those words were. Things that had once seemed so clear to Quinn before he'd left home in search of Michael to warn him about Cecilia. At that point, he'd felt honoured to be given the task, something he had no idea would take up so much of his own life. Somehow that simple task had become complicated and messy.

Pushing against the cane, Cashel got to his feet and shuffled towards Quinn, placing a hand on his shoulder. Cashel softened his tone, "Quinn, you are like a son to me. Promise me that you will not break the Golden Law."

Quinn placed his head in his hands, his fingers tangling in his hands, "I promise, Cashel: I won't break the Golden Law."

Cashel let out a silent breath of relief and returned to his chair in front of the fire.

"I'm tired, Cashel; I think I will sleep now."

Cashel nodded. "The gold will affect you for some time yet; you will need your rest."

Quinn turned to leave and then paused at the base of the wooden steps, "How did you know about...I told you nothing but..."

Cashel smiled the way old men do sometimes and chuckled to himself, turning a moment later to say to Quinn, "You will know one day, if you live as life as long as I."

Feeling defeated, Quinn made his way back up the wooden stairs to the passage. Walking down the passage, he paused; through Mary's ajar door he could see her sound asleep, her hair obscuring her face. His head leaned against the doorframe as he smiled at her. Thoughts turned in his mind and the conflict he felt about the situation continued to rage between his heart and mind. Stepping back, Quinn closed the door before heading to his own bedchamber next to hers.

****

Mary opened her eyes. She looked around the unfamiliar room. Light filtered through the little window. Reaching up, Mary ran her hand over her hair to smooth it down. She searched her mind for the last memory she had; he'd come to the book building, she'd agreed to go, but after that her mind could think of nothing.

A tap at the door and she glanced in its direction. Her heart beat faster; for a moment she envisioned Prater standing on the other side of the door until the image dissipated when she heard a softer voice query, "Mary?"

"Yes?" She didn't know what else to say.

"May I come in?"

"Yes." As the door opened, Mary pulled the blanket that covered her around herself tighter.

"Some new clothes," Quinn spoke as he entered with his arms full of dresses for Mary; he placed them on the chair beside the bed.

"Thank you," Mary replied and glanced at them. They were not like the simple plain brown and black dresses she always wore; she could see a blue one, a pink one, and towards the bottom of the pile, a dark green one. A smile spread over her face at the thought of wearing such dresses.

"I will break the spell, Mary, I promise you that," he uttered the words in a low tone.

"Maybe; there are ways to have it broken aren't there?"

Quinn nodded. "I'll leave you be."

His hand touched the door frame when Mary spoke again, "Quinn." He looked back over his shoulder at her. "You said I called for you, but I didn't."

"Yes, you did...with the stone. I didn't want to leave you without an escape. You must have held the stone at some point and..." he smiled at Mary.

"Is that why you came back?"

Quinn's smile faltered and he looked at his feet. "I felt responsible for what happened; you thought you were saving a dragon after all."

Mary smiled. "And instead I got a sorcerer for my trouble."

"About the binding..." Quinn waited to see if Mary wanted to speak of it. She hadn't been keen on the topic since she had rescued him. When she didn't object, Quinn ventured to continue, "...Why Michael?"

Mary sighed and the smiled faded from her face. "Bit ironic really, I did the calculations wrong, I thought it was fifteen, not sixteen."

"How did..."

"His life was at stake; it wasn't hard to bargain." Mary sighed before continuing, "Quinn, I never felt anything for Michael, not in that way. I wanted to leave Tiani. I wanted to see more of this kingdom, to live. I love books, reading, but I felt suffocated in Tiani; it's such a small place with so few people. I think I felt that if I held onto the dragon then maybe dreams would come true."

"And now?"

"Now? I have no idea. I feel a bit lost."

Quinn nodded in understanding and then left the room.

With Quinn gone, Mary pushed the blankets back to see that she still wore the dress from the day before. Reaching into the pocket, she pulled out the stone. It was cool to the touch, and she wondered if Quinn had told the truth about it. She had admired it, looked at it, and even thought of Quinn, but called him? Mary shook her head and placed the stone onto the little wooden table next to the bed.

Taking the steps two at a time, Quinn's moment of bliss disappeared upon seeing the stern stare from Cashel who was waiting for him at the bottom of the stairs. Normally he would have proceeded with caution, but his mind had been made up, and he had no desire to discuss it with Cashel.

"Where are you going?"

"To do something!"

"Quinn, we settled this last night!" The last word was accentuated by a forceful tap of his walking stick on the wooden floor.

"I promised I would not break the Golden Law – that was all," Quinn replied as he pushed past Cashel.

"So, what are you going to do then? Huh?"

Quinn paused at the front door, contemplating on whether to tell his mentor what had occurred to him during his sleepless night. He knew Cashel would figure it out on his own in time, just like he knew everything else, but by the time he worked it out, the deed would be done.

"I'm going to make a deal."

"Quinn…!" the rest of the sentence faded away as the magic moved Quinn away from his house and towards the mountains that were rumoured to be the resting place of the Dragon Council.

****

Quinn had walked around the plateau several times. He'd cast the summoning spell he remembered from his final year at the Academy to call them forth, and still he stood there alone. Each passing second gave him more time to think over the decision, and more time for the five years of schooling to try and poke holes in his plan.

"Why did you come here?" the voice boomed, and the earth shook as a large dragon landed on the plateau. Quinn stood firm. "You know we've been watching you, waiting for you to go back where you came from. We have no plans to make nice with a sorcerer."

"I have come to make an agreement, a deal of sorts," Quinn replied.

A rush of air encircled Quinn as the large red dragon flapped its wings before tucking them at its side. Quinn felt a little intimidated as the crouched dragon cast a shadow over him. He tried to exhale slowly to maintain his stance by calming his nerves; still his feet betrayed him by shuffling and his fingers gripped the leg of his pants. The dragon's yellow eyes were firmly trained on him.

"A deal? You, a sorcerer, want to make a deal?" a smile passed over the dragon's face. "I'm intrigued so I will not eat you...at the moment anyway. I am Jharobi, representative of the Dragon Council. Speak."

"I wish to ask for a binding spell to be broken."

The dragon's head cocked to one side. "And the reason you ask for this?"

"There is no love in the binding and both parties wish for it to be broken," Quinn replied, pleased that the reason spoke the truth for both Mary and Michael.

"Any other reasons?"

Quinn shifted uncomfortably on the spot, his feet causing a cloud of dust to cover his boots. His eyes wandered away from the dragon's for a moment, but he found himself staring at the large claws more intimidating than Jharobi's face.

"You seem as though you are close to breaking the Golden Law, sorcerer."

Quinn rolled his eyes at the suggestion. He wished everyone would stop reminding him about the Golden Law. He knew all too well about the Golden Law and everything it stood for, but still, at the moment, he resented it even existed. If it hadn't been for the Golden Law, the Academy would never have charged him with stopping his sister, and perhaps he just might have had a life instead of spending ten years following Cecilia's every move.

"Why do you all keep saying that? How would you have any idea how close I am to breaking something like that?"

"When you get as old as I am, sorcerer, you tend to know more things. You'll never be as old as I am, seeing as how we dragons live much longer lives, but perhaps you will live long enough to understand."

"You sound like my mentor," Quinn growled and ran his hands through his hair.

Jharobi laughed. "He must an old sorcerer to understand then; you would do well to listen to him.

Did you know, Quinn, that we dragons can see into the heart? We can read what lies within, although normally sorcerers' are a little harder to read, a bit foggier. Not a skill that sorcerers have, though the accuracy of your technology does surpass ours at the moment."

"So. then you know my other reason for the request."

"It is a request I didn't think you would ask for."

"I don't ask for myself, but for her."

"It is no secret that dragons and sorcerers don't like each other. When the Great War ended, specific rules that both sides had to abide by were agreed upon, none of them more important than the Golden Law." Jharobi paused. "What price will you pay for the freedom of Mary from the binding?"

"Anything," Quinn replied, his gaze locked onto Jharobi's.

"I believe that you mean that, sorcerer. I will grant your request, but it will have a price."

Quinn waited for the dragon to continue.

"I can't take away your power as you know, another of the rules, but I will assume you have dared to approach the Dragon Council instead of the Sorcery Council because there is more to this than maybe even we are aware. If you choose, Quinn, with your consent, I can facilitate the process where you can give up your power."

"You want me to hand over my power, my family's magic?" A higher price than even Quinn had expected.

"Exactly. You care for this girl, but I want to know how far you are willing to go to prove that you care more deeply. Caring for someone, sorcerer, and loving them are two different things."

Jharobi curled his tail around his body but the end continued to flick back and forth as he stared at Quinn, waiting for the answer.

Quinn debated the two sides of the deal, especially the consequences. "Without my magic how will I stop my sister? How can I break the spell...?"

Jharobi blew a puff of smoke from his nostrils and replied, "*That,* sorcerer, is not my problem. Are you willing to prove your love? You would be mortal, after all, and free to pursue your feelings without fear of retribution from the Golden Law."

Quinn felt his heart beat quicken. His hand reached up and pressed against his chest to attempt to steady the pace with the aid of magic but to no avail. He could break the binding, but then he would not be able to break the spell on Mary and would have no way stopping Cecilia from herself breaking the Golden Law – a no-win situation loomed before him.

"Well, sorcerer, do we have a deal?"

Quinn broke his eye contact with the dragon. He wanted to break the binding more than anything, however, it would serve only to have his sister break the Golden Law and the dragons declare war again for breaching the agreement.

"Decisions of the heart are never easy, sorcerer. You must choose between peace in this land and the love within your heart for both of those ladies."

"Both?" Quinn paused. Jharobi was right. This wasn't just about Mary but about Cecelia too. "Why? Why do I have to choose? Why does the Golden Law even need to exist any longer? The Great War was a long time ago. Would it be truly terrible if a sorcerer were to be bound to a mortal?"

Jharobi rose up from his resting position so that he towered over Quinn. Quinn's eyes glanced to the side to see how much room he had to move around. The comfort of knowing the dragon couldn't kill him didn't abate the fear Jharobi had created in his mind.

"You know why, sorcerer! It is what you have fought to prevent your sister from doing all these years. If a sorcerer were ever to bind to a mortal again, it would mean a powerful alliance, one that dragons could not beat even if good sorcerers were to join us. It was what started the Great War in the first place!"

"So, because I stand for good, I must pay the same price as the wicked?"

"We pay the price also, sorcerer. Do not fool yourself into believing that you are the only one who has been forced to make this decision."

Jharobi spread his wings, ready to leave, when Quinn objected, "I have not told you my decision."

"You didn't need to." A rush of wind and the space before Quinn became empty. The dragon knew he would do the right thing for all, not just himself. Quinn walked over to the edge of the plateau; below him the Great Forest spread out at the base of the mountain.

"Why?" The word echoed across the treetops as Quinn clenched his hands into fists.

Memories of the years he'd spend all for The Academy and their orders; orders that had persisted well beyond schooling. He stared out at the landscape, his jaw clenched. Trapped by his training into doing what was right for everyone else.

He kicked his foot at the ground and sent rocks cascading in all directions. At his feet a larger stone sat and he prodded it with the toe of his shoe. Quinn bent down and his fingers curled around the rock, the sharp edges dug into his skin as he gripped it. He stood up and swung his arm back before he launched it into the air.

"I hate all of this! I've had enough! Do you hear me? I hate it all! I want a life for once. I hate all of it!"

The rock disappeared from view. Quinn shook his head before he sat on the ground and pulled his knees up to his chest. He rested his head on his knees, breathed deeply, and tried to calm the conflicted thoughts in his mind.

****

When Quinn arrived back home, he noticed Cashel's absence, but Mary sat by the blazing fire in Cashel's wicker seat. A blanket was wrapped firmly around her shoulders, and she'd tucked her feet underneath her body. Her eyes followed the crackling flames as they danced above the wooden logs that were slowly turning into charcoal. Quinn noticed she wore one of the dresses he had given her that morning – the dark green one.

"Mary," Quinn said as he walked past her to sit in his usual chair, "Did you see an elderly man?"

"I've seen no one since I last saw you." She paused. "You've been gone some time. Where have you been?"

"Nowhere special."

Silence descended on the pair as both watched the flames intensely. Quinn searched his mind for something to say but the conversation with Jharobi still niggled at his mind.

"I told him about Cecilia," Mary whispered.

"Huh?" Quinn looked over at Mary, his own thoughts trailing off.

"I told Prater about Cecilia." The flames of the fire continued to flicker and dance; Mary's voice lowered as she added, "I didn't want to, but he had me locked in the cell. I'm sorry, I shouldn't have told him."

"It's okay, Mary, really. Don't give it another thought," Quinn said soothingly, but Mary bit her lip in response.

"What's going to happen now?"

"I don't know, Mary." Tracing his right index finger in a circle on the wooden arm of the chair, Quinn felt utterly helpless, even a little useless. "No harm will come to you here, Mary, I can promise that. I know I've made you a lot of promises, but I keep my word, Mary. My sister will choose a new man and my task will start again, but as long as you want to be here, you have a home."

Quinn felt the closeness to Mary; he only had to reach out his hand and he would be able to touch hers. *After all,* he told himself, *it isn't like I can break the Golden Law at the moment anyway.*

"Mary."

She didn't respond.

"Mary."

Mary turned her head and looked over at Quinn and smiled.

"It will all work out." Quinn reached over and placed his hand over hers on the arm rest of her chair. She looked down at his hand. Quinn thought she might pull away for a moment but relaxed when she placed her free hand over his.

Quinn moved his chair magically closer to Mary and reached up with his left hand to cup her face; in response she closed her eyes.

"Thank you for coming back, Quinn," she whispered.

Quinn moved closer until his lips were near her ear.

"It will all work out," the words were whispered, and he lightly kissed her cheek.

Quinn knew that he had done more than Cashel would approve of – Cashel who could appear at any moment, Cashel who would know all regardless of being told nothing. In spite of those thoughts, Quinn kissed her cheek again and again, moving closer to her lips with each one.

Just a kiss, the words kept revolving around Quinn's mind even as he held tightly onto Mary. He didn't want to let her go; he certainly didn't want to stop. *Just one kiss,* but he knew as well as an observer would that a string of sustained kisses hardly counted as one. At length, Quinn eased his grip on Mary's shoulders.

"I'll keep you safe, Mary." Quinn whispered as he rested his forehead against hers, closing his own eyes to help calm the debate he felt inside between his head and heart.

As Quinn settled down next to Mary, with his right arm still over her shoulders, they sat in silence until she fell asleep. Quinn carried her up to her room and laid her on the bed, covering her with the blankets. She didn't stir at all. When he returned downstairs, he found his mentor warming himself in his usual chair, which had been returned to its usual place. Quinn sat back down in his chair, contemplating what his mentor might be thinking – and how much he already knew.

"Quinn, what continues to trouble you?" Cashel asked tiredly from beside the young sorcerer.

"I went to the Great Forest to see the dragons."

Quinn's mind had thought of the look of horror that would pass over Cashel's face when he told him, and he hadn't been too far off with his imagination.

"Quinn..."

"I know, Cashel. You don't need to lecture me on the reasons why it was foolish." Cashel closed his open mouth and pursed his lips together. "She's a good person, Cashel. Mary has protected those books, despite it costing her family all their lives..."

"I am curious to know what your request was to the dragons."

Quinn looked over at Cashel, then back to the blazing fire.

"I asked for her to be free from the binding."

"I am surprised to hear that. I did not think that would be your exact request." Cashel paused before continuing, "Mary is a very wholesome girl, and in regards to the books, she has done a fine job...but you have removed her from what she protected, which I am not sure if it would please the dragons. I am thinking the price would have been high to have the binding removed."

"It was too high."

"Gold? Riches?" Quinn looked over at Cashel at the suggestion. "Not everything is told to all sorcerers; you should understand that by now. Amongst the elite sorcerers and members of the Council it is well know that dragons have a love of glittery objects. Some even believe that dragons purposely bargain for gold with sorcerers just to see them in such a weakened state."

"I've never heard that."

"Like I said, Quinn, it's not common knowledge; it comes from knowledge gained by the Council having to clean up messes like you are in with your sister. Anyway, you keep that to yourself, otherwise I'll find myself in trouble with them, too. So, what did they ask for then?"

"My magic."

"Oh." Cashel paused. "Well, I'm pleased that you had the sense to not do something that foolish at least. You must leave things as they are, Quinn." A moment of silence fell.

"Why do you think Cecilia took away her ability to read?"

"Cecilia is a smart woman: she knows that the best way to crush a person is to take away what they value the most, and for Mary that meant her reading."

"How can I make it up to Mary? I can't teach her – I don't know how..."

"You must not keep Mary here, Quinn. Find her somewhere safe – in one of the cities maybe? She'll find her own way, and you can continue to find yours. You'll need to report to the Sorcery Council soon."

"Yeah, I know. I have to think more about this Cashel."

CHAPTER EIGHTEEN

Mary sat by the fireplace in the cold. The fire had long since died down and she sat looking at where it once burned. Outside the sun shone brightly through the windows as she thought of home and of the books and of reading.

"Young lady: that is *my* chair."

Mary turned at the sound of the stern and unfamiliar voice. An old man stood with a walking stick in one hand that he had pointed directly at her.

"I'm sorry, I didn't know…" her words trailed off. Hurriedly, she got out of the chair and awkwardly stood off to the side, contemplating whether she would be allowed to sit in the other chair.

The elderly man gingerly made his way towards the now vacant chair and eased himself into it; momentarily his eyes closed before he turned his attention back to Mary. Her hand lightly touched the back of the chair and her fingers tapped against it.

"I am Cashel. I have heard a great deal about you Mary. My apprentice feels that he owes you. Sit down in the chair."

Mary watched as the man tapped the floor with his stick and the fire was once again burning brightly; she knew he must be a sorcerer, just a very old one.

Once she sat down the old man continued, "You are a danger to Quinn the longer you stay here. He has a difficult challenge ahead of him, no one should have to quarrel with their family, but I can't change any of that." Cashel turned and looked over at Mary. "You distract Quinn. You cause him to change his priorities. He must not be distracted at this point."

"What would you have me do?" Mary whispered; she had a feeling that she already knew the answer to the question he had just asked.

"You need to leave, go somewhere," Cashel paused, keeping Mary in his sight. "Don't go back to Tiani but go somewhere safe – start a new life without the burden of words and reading."

"But what would I do?"

"Young lady, do you expect me to solve all your problems!" his voice boomed, and Mary sat frozen in fright. Cashel looked at her for a moment before he sunk further into his own seat. "Mary, you are a sweet girl, but you are a danger to a sorcerer – almost all mortals are. Pack a few things now; I'll find a place to leave you."

"Can I at least think about it?"

"There isn't time, young lady," Cashel paused and looked over at Mary. "Quinn would like you to stay but there is more going on here that what you are aware of. Things that have been in motion for years need to be concluded and rules must be followed."

Mary's eyes found the wooden floor and she knew that he wasn't giving her a choice in the matter. She felt disappointed to be leaving the safety of Quinn and his house, feelings swirled inside of her. On her hand, she traced the binding mark with her right hand's index finger. She remembered the feel of Quinn's lips – the feelings that had bubbled inside her that she had always wanted to feel. Quinn was so close... yet still out of reach as long as the binding existed. Mary sighed.

"I'll go and pack."

Mary left the room with a heavy heart and headed towards the stairs. Every time her foot stepped up, she felt less inclined to continue; she hadn't realised that Quinn shared his home with someone who had the power to make such a decision.

In her room, Mary looked at the dresses that Quinn had brought to her. She didn't want to leave them behind – they were nicer than anything she had ever had, but she also wondered if it would be right to take them with her. Shaking her head in frustration, Mary looked around the room for a bag to put her things in.

"There's got to be something here," Mary muttered, as she got down on the floor and peered under the bed. To her satisfaction she found a bag – albeit a rather dusty and forgotten one.

She gave the bag a solid shake and dust rose from it like before it infiltrated her lungs and she began to cough. Her hand waved in front of her as she tried to clear the air. As she steadied her breathing she folded the dresses and placed them into the bag. When she turned to the table beside the bed she saw the trinkets and placed them in the bag too. Mary's gaze fell onto the little green-blue stone that sat alone and innocent. Her hand hovered over it, contemplating whether she should take it or not.

Will the old man know if I take it? If I take it, will I be tempted to hold it again, the way that caused Quinn to know I was thinking of him and wanted him to come back?

The previous night's kiss again flashed in Mary's mind, and instinctively she reached and brushed her lips with her fingertips. Mary pursed her lips together and knitted her brows in frustration. She knew for sure that she wanted to take the stone with her, but she also knew that if she did take it, she *would* want to hold it and *would* want to be near Quinn again. The hovering hand above the stone transformed into a fist and Mary lowered it until the arm and hand hung limp beside her body; *best not to have the temptation.*

****

"Mary?" Quinn knocked on the door. "Mary?"

When there was no answer, Quinn opened the door. The bed was neatly made, but Mary's things were missing from the bedside table. Walking towards it, he saw that something remained on the table – the calling stone. Snatching the stone from the table, he turned his head and noticed that all of Mary's clothes were all gone too.

"Cashel!"

Running noisily down the steps two at a time, Quinn found his mentor in his usual seat by the fire; he looked peaceful and happy. Cashel's eyes were closed, despite the noise, and he appeared to be in no hurry to open them.

"Where is Mary? What have you done?" Quinn demanded.

At length, Cashel opened his eyes, but his attention was on the fire and not Quinn who stood behind him at the base of the stairs. "She's gone, Quinn: Mary is gone."

"Where? Tell me where."

"I can't, Quinn."

Quinn walked over to his mentor and squatted down beside him, looking him in the eyes.

"Tell me where Mary is."

Cashel raised his hand to Quinn's pleading face. "I told you, I can't – I don't know where she is."

"How can that be? The only way to leave this house is by magic – you must know where she is!" Quinn clenched his fingers into a ball and tried to keep his temper in check.

"Really, Quinn? Your naivety is disappointing. I told you I didn't know where she was and that was the truth." Cashel turned away from his apprentice.

With Cashel's attention on the fire, Quinn sat down in the chair beside him and leaned forward. He heard his mentor sigh and looked back over at him in hope.

"I must be getting too old for all this. Look, Quinn, I asked her to think of a place that she wanted to go and then I spirited her there."

Quinn's hands relaxed and he ran his fingers through his hair. It hadn't been the information he had wanted to hear. "But she could be anywhere."

"It is for the best, Quinn. You have more to learn – Cecilia has likely already chosen her new target – you can't allow Mary to interfere with the greater good at stake here."

"But I won't see her again."

Cashel sighed. "Quinn, I'm…it's for the best. Everything I've ever done was with you in mind and the best for you. I would never want you to think that I would injure you in such a way."

The palm of Quinn's hand rested on his forehead. He contemplated whether to keep pushing but Cashel had never been one to hide things from him.

"I made something for you, before Mary left; go to your bedchamber."

Standing up with a heavy and sad heart, Quinn looked in the direction of his bedchamber. He had not expected Cashel to have made him a gift – such things were rare. Glancing at his mentor, he turned and walked up the stairs, more slowly than he had descended them, thinking nothing could lift his spirits.

In his bedchamber, Quinn found a small bundle on his bed, wrapped in brown paper and string. Quinn magically unknotted the string and then unfolded the brown paper. Turning the object over, it was a frame, and inside was a lifelike picture of Mary and she was smiling. Sitting on the bed, Quinn held the picture in his hand and traced his finger over Mary's face. Quinn had always believed in fate and he had foolishly begun to believe that Mary was part of it.

CHAPTER NINETEEN

Mary stared at the large manor house that loomed before her. An enormous stone building with an elegant red tiled roof and windows that were each framed in the same style timber with shutters on either side. The whiteness of the walls and pale blue trim seemed out of place against the picturesque background of mountains and trees.

Nervously, Mary stood at the door, unsure of whether to knock or not. When Cashel had asked her to think of a place she had instead thought of a person – and then found herself standing right where she now waited. Raising her hand and clenching her fingers into a fist, she prepared to knock on the door.

"Is there something you want?"

Mary heard the familiar voice behind her and hesitated at turning around.

"I said: is there something you want?"

After lowering her hand, Mary slowly turned around to face him – it was now or never.

"Mary?" Michael stared at her with his mouth agape. His shook his head and laughed before his eyes slowly went back on her and his smile faded.

"I have nowhere else to go."

Michael continued to stare at Mary. Self-consciously, she reached up and pulled on her hair that hung in a single ponytail. When he continued to say nothing, Mary's hand smoothed down the dress she wore.

"Sorry, you look different, really different. I'm not sure what to say to be honest."

Mary looked at Michael. He had improved in appearance from when she had last seen him; his cheeks were no longer drawn and the cuts and bruises had healed without leaving any marks that she could see. His clothes she had last seen him in had been replaced with black trousers and a crisp white shirt – Mary had only seen people from the large cities wearing such outfits.

"I..." Mary's mind couldn't come up with an easy way to explain why she had landed there. She felt angry towards Cashel for not giving her a chance to properly consider what he said; she wanted to kick herself for thinking of Michael but conceded it might have been worse: *What if I'd thought of Prater?* It sent a shiver down her spine.

"You expect me to what?"

"I have nowhere to go…I thought…" Mary paused in her stuttered speech and lowered her head, feeling foolish. "You once offered…I thought…"

The suddenness of the door opening behind her caused Mary to jump in fright and her attention diverted towards the noise. In the doorway, a middle-aged woman with greying hair stood. Her dress, made from exquisite red fabric, fell without a wrinkle to her ankles, and her hair was in fancy braids that curled into buns at the base of her neck.

"Who are you?"

Mary smoothed her dress again. Even if the dress didn't need it, her hands certainly benefited from the action. She unclasped her hands in front of her and brushed some stray hair away from her face as she searched for the words she had practised in her mind.

The woman reached out and grabbed Mary's hand, turning her towards her and leaning forward to look over her glasses. "Oh my, you're the girl bound to Michael."

Mary gulped, wondering if the woman thought that a good or bad idea, but as she watched, a smile came over her face and she pulled Mary to her for a hug. The tightness and joy in the hug felt foreign to Mary, and she stood stiffly until the woman pushed her slightly away to have another look at her.

"Oh dear, you must come in, come in." The woman glanced past Mary at Michael, raising her eyebrows and encouraging him to follow with her beckoning hand. "I am so happy to meet you, my dear; Michael has told us nothing…"

Mary felt overwhelmed by the woman as she ushered her inside and into a meeting room. As the woman sat down, she beckoned Mary to join her on the soft comfortable looking seat with her hand.

She shuffled her feet for a moment before Mary walked over to the woman and sat down on the edge of the seat. It was very different from the hard, wooden chairs in the book building, and she wondered if it were possible to be swallowed by furniture.

"I'm Sallie, Michael's mother. I have been waiting so long to meet you. What's your name, dear?"

"Mary."

"Mary. Mary, I am so happy you have finally come here. Michael told us nothing when he came back, and my husband and I supposed that...well we didn't really know to be honest...but now you have come here at last."

"I have nowhere else to go."

Sallie looked perplexed at Mary's comment. "What do you mean 'nowhere else to go'?"

"Mother..." Mary looked back at the doorway and saw that Michael stood there with his arms crossed in front of his chest, interrupting the whiteness of his shirt.

"Don't you *mother* me, young man! You tell us nothing of your wife, and you act as though she didn't even exist, and now you have the nerve to *mother* me now that she has finally come here to meet us?"

Michael's lip twitched in annoyance. When he glanced over at her, she sensed he wanted her to give an explanation of the binding. Mary gulped in response before she turned to look back at Sallie who stared at her son with deep lines across her forehead.

"Mary, are you pleased to see Michael again? Tell me about your family."

"Ma'am, please. You are very kind, but I am only asking for a place to stay and food. The circumstance surrounding Michael and I becoming bound is…is…rather awkward."

Sallie looked at Mary; the smile that she had kept on Mary since opening the door faltered. "What do you mean?"

Mary glanced in Michael's direction. His eyebrows were raised, and he seemed to be waiting to hear the explanation as well. She had supposed that Michael would have at least explained *something* to his family but that seemed unlikely given Sallie's reaction.

"Mary?"

Mary looked down at her clasped hands that held tightly onto the bag. "Ma'am, Michael came to my village, and he was in a bit of a…a…predicament. You see our village leader, Master Prater, thought Michael to be a dragon…and so…and so…I rescued him from the cells before he was to be hung."

"What a lovely girl you were to do such a thing!" The smile of relief appeared on Sallie's face, and she relaxed a little more into her chair.

"Wait, Mother – there's more," Michael interrupted. Sallie stiffened again.

"The thing is I made Michael agree to be bound to me...before...before I would rescue him."

Again, the smile faltered.

Mary found maintaining any form of eye contact with Sallie or Michael difficult and focused on her clasped hands in her lap. The silence that befell the room felt never-ending, and Mary wondered if she would be welcomed at all now that Sallie knew the truth about the binding.

"So, he agreed, and you rescued him?"

Mary nodded.

"And then you went and abandoned her!" Sallie stood up, her finger jabbed the air in front of her as she faced her son. In response, Michael raised his hands and took a step backwards.

Mary found herself compelled to stand and defend him. "No ma'am, that's not how it was."

Sallie paused – her finger still pointed menacingly at Michael.

"I made Michael leave me behind."

"Why would you do such a thing?"

Mary sat back on the comfortable seat and looked up at Sallie before looking at Michael.

"I realised that I had made a mistake."

Sallie lowered her hand and sat back down. Her eyes flicked back and forth between Mary and Michael; she let out a sigh.

"You knew that my son was already promised to be bound to another?"

"Yes, he told me."

"But you made him bind to you anyway?"

"Yes."

Sallie turned to Michael, "She's honest; I'll give her that."

The room was enveloped in silence again, and after a couple of minutes had passed, Mary dared to look up. Sallie appeared deep in thought as she sucked in the side of her cheek, her mouth moving around intermittently. Mary looked away from Sallie, afraid she would burst out laughing at the sight.

"Well, my children: what is done is done and there is nothing we can do to change what happened in the past. Mary, you are welcome to stay here as long as you wish and you are welcome – I'll have a spare room made up for you, if you wish."

"I would appreciate that."

Sallie only smiled in response before rising and leaving the room while she called out for a servant girl, to prepare a new room. From her position on the seat, Mary's eyes followed Sallie until she disappeared from view, leaving her alone with Michael. Mary looked over at him and contemplated what to say but glanced away; her eyes focused out of the window that faced onto the front grounds of the property the manor occupied.

"I am sorry..." Mary said, but when she turned to look, she saw that she was the only one in the room.

****

Mary had been in the company of Michael's family for two days. Mostly she had walked the gardens or kept to her room. There were no books to read, and while Sallie had attempted to coax her into doing needlepoint, Mary had politely declined. Having nothing to do though spurred Mary's thoughts to changing her life again. This time she knew that Quinn wouldn't be there to try and fix things, and with no Prater to avoid, Mary almost considered it to be a second chance.

No, I don't need someone to break Cecilia's spell, Mary thought as she dressed the morning of the third day in the house. *If I want to have a life, then I need to change what I'm doing; I need to take control of my own life.*

Michael's mother had been very friendly and welcoming. She knew she had chosen to come here to this place for a reason and it wasn't because of Michael – it wasn't Tiani and it wasn't Haversy.

"Could you tell me how to get into the nearest town?" Mary asked as she sat down for breakfast.

"I'll have the carriage take you in." Sallie looked up from her own breakfast and smiled.

"I don't want to be any bother…" Mary's eyes fell on the unoccupied seat at the head of the table. She had expected to have met Michael's father by now. However the maid had told her he had been away on business for a few weeks and wouldn't be returning until the end of the month. Michael sat opposite Mary at the table and as she observed him for a reaction, she wondered if Michael resembled his father at all.

"Don't be silly, Mary, you are family; it is no bother at all," Sallie paused and looked over at her son who sat opposite Mary at the table. "Michael, why don't you escort Mary into town?"

"I have other plans."

"Michael," the sharp tone Sallie used confirmed she required, not requested it.

Mary felt uncomfortable and preferred to go into town on her own. With her newfound determination, Mary had no plans to stay with Michael's family indefinitely, but until she could read again, she thought it would be the best place to be. *Plus,* Mary reminded herself, *Prater will not be able to find me here.*

****

Sitting on the carriage watching the countryside pass by intrigued Mary. She had never been in a carriage before and hadn't spent much time around horses either. The scenic countryside that surrounded Michael's home had quickly faded away into many little houses dotted along the roads. She noted that the closer they got to the town, the larger and better constructed the buildings became and the more manicured the gardens grew.

"Where did you want to go?" Michael sounded impatient in his tone as he sat next to Mary.

"To the book building in town." Mary paused and nervously rubbed her thumb over the back of her other hand. "You need not wait for me; I can make my own way back."

Michael urged the horses on and after a while asked, "Why did you come here Mary?"

"Like I said, I have nowhere to go."

"You seem different than...than before."

Mary ignored the comment and continued to look at her hands. Finally she replied, "There's something I need to do. I know you don't care for me and that is fine. All I ask is for a roof over my head and food – nothing more. I am trying to have the binding broken; I will do everything I can to have it broken."

Michael looked over at Mary as her gaze remained on her hands. "Not much point in breaking it now. Cecilia, the girl I was going to be bound to, well, I haven't seen her since I got back. I heard that she already knows about you...and...well, I don't know...everything is somehow different now...I think."

"I am sorry. I didn't intend for anyone to be hurt. I just wanted some good luck."

For the rest of the distance they travelled in silence. Michael stopped the carriage outside of a building which looked similar to the one in Tiani. The façade was tall and appeared to be of at least three storeys in height, built from stone that had been so smoothly polished the sun's light reflected off the surface. The large windows of the ground floor were patterned with different panes of glass – much like the small glass pane above the door in Tiani – but there were no dragons to be seen, and they were much more elaborate, with scenes of the forest life in one and the sea in another. Mary dismounted from the carriage and Michael urged the horses on and the carriage continued down the street.

Walking through the main door, the book building opened up to be far larger than the one back in Tiani. Instead of one main room there were several and all were visible from the entrance.

"Greetings, young lady," an elderly man, leaning heavily on a walking stick and who reminded Mary a little of Yansa, came up to her with a smile on his face. "What brings you to the book building today?"

"Teach me how to read."

The elderly man's eyebrows lifted but a smile spread over his face. "To read? Well, young lady, that is not something I have requested of me very often. In fact, I do believe you are only the fourth person to ever ask me that. Of course I will teach you. I'm Elkan, the book-keeper."

"I'm Mary."

"The young lady bound to Michael?"

Mary had not realised that others would know of that. Elkan chucked, "This is a small city, my child, word travels fast. You will be an example to the rest of this city to learn to read, especially considering the influence that Michael's family has here."

Mary picked up a book from the nearest table. At least being amongst books would give her a chance to locate the one of dragon spells, and if she could learn to read again then maybe she could accomplish anything.

"Did you wish to start today?"

Mary looked over at Elkan and nodded, "Yes, very much so."

Being surrounded by the walls of books, Mary felt happy; it almost felt like home.

CHAPTER
TWENTY

Quinn eyed Cecilia from across the road as she smiled coyly at a gentleman. Cecilia was dressed in a very fine gown of green fabric; a line of silver embroidery danced across the hem of the skirt and sleeves. An unusual accompaniment she wore was a beaded snood – something usually seen only in the southern region – a thought that momentarily brought his thoughts to Mary.

As Quinn continued to observe Cecilia with much delight he saw the brief glower on her face. He turned his thoughts to his time at the Academy when had been first charged with the assignment regarding Cecilia. The assignment had been given to him by the Sorcery Council which had become concerned when they received information that Cecilia had begun to court Michael, a human. That day, Quinn's own plans ceased and the assignment became the future he now knew.

Cecilia smiled sweetly at another man and Quinn laughed to himself.

"Excuse me, Miss." The gentleman tipped his hat and stepped around her before continuing down the street – the fifth gentleman she had failed to impress that morning, and the frustration of the lack of success showed on her face.

Crossing the road, Quinn approached his sister and tapped her on her shoulder. "Perhaps you should just give up?"

"Why, baby brother, what brings you here? Don't you have better things to do with your time?"

"Thought I'd see the city by the sea myself; haven't been here for a long time."

Cecilia and Quinn walked side by side down the paved street.

"I wouldn't have thought the city was your style – out of the way backward villages have always been more suited to you." Cecilia paused to look at her brother. "So I guess you are keeping a close eye on that stupid girl?"

Quinn looked forward, closed his eyes and took in a deep breath of fresh sea air. "Of course."

"Liar!" chided Cecilia with a smile. "You never were much good at it – beat you every time when we were kids. I doubt that not having her around was your choosing brother, no, that would be Cashel's doing. Did he get a little nervous that his prodigy could actually consider breaking the Golden Law?"

"Cecilia..."

"That's it, isn't it, brother?" A laugh uttered from Cecilia's mouth, "I thought so when I saw you with that girl in the book building. There was something just a little bit different about you from when we had last crossed paths. We are not so different, Quinn."

"But what we want isn't for the same reason."

"What do reasons have to do with anything?"

"Motives are everything, sister, and you know it."

"And yet we both find ourselves in the same place – the wrong side of the Golden Law."

"Can't we bury this? I am tired of fighting with you."

"But this is us. Even when we were kids, we fought – I just learnt to fight for what I wanted instead of fighting for what others wanted," Cecilia paused, her hand lightly reached out to touch Quinn's arm. "You need to decide what it is that you want, Quinn. You've chased me for ten years because other people told you it was you that had to stop me – think about what you have missed out on…"

"I can't be selfish like that."

"Why not? Who says that we can't be selfish once or twice in our lifetime?"

"The Academy…"

"Oh, don't get me started on that place! Quinn, listen to yourself."

"Nothing will change, Cecilia. Mary is bound to Michael…the price is too high to break it…"

Cecilia looked at her brother. "What price is too high?"

"Nothing, I just mean that…death is too high a price to break the binding."

"Death? Baby brother I do believe you are hiding something from me." A smile passed over Cecilia's lips. "No worries though, I am working on that one myself."

"You know that you can't take the life of a mortal…"

"Now did I say that I was going to do that? Tut-tut, baby brother, why do you always think the worst of me? I want more power, not anything at all." Cecilia let go of Quinn who continued to look intently at the paving stone that they stood on. "You are so focused on me that you never see the big picture – that is why you will never win against me."

Cecilia continued walking, and Quinn remained where he stood, watching her glide along the pavement, her shoes clicking as she walked. Her words lingered though, and Quinn wondered what the big picture could be...

Moving into the trees, Quinn waved his hand. A sparkle of blue light surrounded his hand before it spread out, enveloping him fully. The familiar experience had no impact on him as Cecilia's words haunted his thoughts. When the magic settled, he looked around at where he stood; back in the book building in Tiani. He sighed with relief that his planned entrance within the walls of the building had been successful but stood frozen as he listened for any sounds, just in case.

After wandering around downstairs in the eerie silence that permeated the atmosphere, Quinn sighed. He would have been able to see more had he been able to light a candle, but with the darkness outside he certainly didn't want to attract the attention of a certain village member. All around him, Quinn noted, were piles of books abandoned on the floor and tables. It was an odd sight to see the books disturbed – especially after putting them back on the shelves before leaving with Mary. He raised his eyebrows at the thought of what the dragons would think if they saw the building as it was. For the briefest of moments, he thought about putting the books back on the shelves. A half-smile played on Quinn's lips at Prater's reaction upon seeing the books back where they belonged.

With such a thought still in his mind, Quinn decided it would be best to remove the temptation and walked upstairs. At the top of the stairs, in front of the only door off the landing, Quinn paused. He knew that there was really no reason to go into the room – it wasn't as if there would be something, or rather someone, there – but despite this his hand found the handle and turned it anyway.

As he closed the door silently behind himself, Quinn surveyed the room. A layer of dust had already formed over the few objects in the room. The room felt oddly cold, sad, or perhaps it felt that way because of its emptiness. Opposite the room was Mary's bed, neatly made as if she was busy downstairs with the books. Quinn turned, realising the room contained no personal possessions.

The quilt, it was a sudden, odd thought, but the quilt did indeed signify some care and life had existed in the room. Walking over to the bed, Quinn lowered himself down onto the quilt. The index finger of his right hand traced over the stitches. The room was empty, Quinn knew that, yet oddly he had a sense of Mary – as if part of her still lingered in the room.

Another sigh. Quinn knew his magical house was far superior, and yet it was simply a house that he had created as part of his training with Cashel – an ideal house, and up until that moment he'd never considered anything else – certainly not anything real.

****

"What news?" Cashel asked Quinn as he entered the room through the front door. With Mary gone he might have just as easily appeared directly in the room, but Quinn had become accustomed to entering through the door – it made him feel less like a sorcerer and more human.

"What?"

"News, Quinn: what news?"

Quinn looked away from his mentor as he walked further into the room, contemplating how much he should tell and how long he could conceal the truth from Cashel.

"Cecilia hasn't been at her house near Riejan for some time; it has been all but abandoned," Quinn replied and took off his black coat and draped it over the back of his chair before he settled down in front of the fire. As he closed his eyes, he felt an immense tiredness come over him and felt no motivation to do anything else for the day.

"You have been gone some time; surely you have more news?"

"She's gone from the Great Forest – I traced her as far as the Great Sea, but I don't know where she has gone. Cecilia could be across the waters or living next door." Quinn didn't mention the conversation they had.

"You must not give up." Cashel leaned forward in his chair with all the urgency of a man close to death. "You are close, Quinn, so close to defeating your sister. You have come so far and I know you have sacrificed a lot, but the knowledge we have, the power that sorcerers hold, the Council continue to search for an end to this matter. Why it's possible they might even find a way to take her power away or destroy her."

Quinn opened his eyes, but his face told of a dejected sorcerer who had lost his purpose, lost his will. "I don't want to destroy her, Cashel! Cecilia is still my sister – perhaps she is not as bad as I once thought."

"Pfff! Are you now going to sit there and claim that perhaps Cecilia might actually be in love with Michael? That all she wants is happiness with no ulterior movements! You can't be that naïve! I did not spend years training you to be so ignorant!"

"And what happens when you are gone, Cashel? What will I have? Perhaps Cecilia is a little misguided...but I get it...I get some of where she is coming from."

"Quinn, you are young. Once you have taken care of Cecilia, you will have time on your hands to go to The Academy and meet a sorceress..."

"What if I don't want a sorceress?" the harsh words left Quinn's lips before he had a chance to think about them.

"Quinn!"

Quinn relaxed in his chair. "I like being treated normally. I like not having to compete with shows of power..." Quinn rested his head in his hands.

Memories of his time at The Academy tormented the back of his mind. He had hoped attending the school would provide refuge from thoughts of his missing parents. It did in a way. For two years, he had managed his studies, but then, at only fifteen, the Sorcery Council had given him the task of stopping Cecilia's plans.

He lifted his head and glanced at Cashel. The old man had been ready to leave The Academy when the Sorcery Council asked him to take on an apprentice. Quinn knew he had shelved his own plans to return across the sea to where he had been born. Cashel had no family to return to, having never been bound or had children. As Quinn looked at him he knew that wasn't the future he wanted but one he quite possibly faced if Cecilia's plan couldn't be foiled.

Cashel caught Quinn's eyes. "Perhaps once Cecilia is no longer after the power and when all the dust settles you could see the Council. Who knows, with the talks between them and the Dragon Council maybe there is a way around the rule, maybe something could be done to…with Mary…maybe …"

Quinn smiled briefly in cynicism. "And perhaps there will be a day when the rules and councils are no longer needed."

As Quinn sat there in silence, watching the flames dancing on the wood, he heard Cashel let out a sigh, the kind he'd heard more frequently than in the years before.

"Why have you come back, sorcerer?" Jharobi growled as he landed before Quinn again.

"I agree to your terms," Quinn replied. He felt confident in the decision despite knowing there might be more consequences than just losing his magic, particularly with the Sorcery Council.

"You agree to relinquish your magic?" Surprise permeated Jharobi's tone; he crouched down so that his head rested on his feet.

"Yes." Quinn saw again the look of an amused dragon as he puffed smoke from his nostrils.

"You know that without your agreement I can't take your powers away; I need to be sure that you understand what you are doing," the dragon paused and inclined his head to one side. "You fully understand the consequences of what you are asking?"

"Yes."

The dragon opened his mouth before closing it again. He sat there looking at Quinn for a few moments. "I will ask just once more, sorcerer, do you agree to relinquish your magic in order to break a binding spell?"

"Yes." Quinn stood emotionless before the dragon. He felt that if he let his emotions or thoughts interfere again, he might just leave.

With another puff of smoke, the dragon raised himself up until he sat before Quinn.

"I don't really understand why you are doing this, but I will respect your decision all the same." The dragon spread his wings out before adding, "You have a long walk ahead of you, sorcerer," and with those words, the dragon took off into the sky, vanishing against the sunlight

"What? That's it?" Quinn called after the dragon but Jharobi didn't return. He'd expected something more elaborate than a verbal agreement, though he'd never seen a dragon perform magic before.

Quinn turned around and wondered how he would get back to his house. He hadn't considered that he wouldn't be able to magically locate it, and now it would take several weeks to reach. He knew he would need to pass through many villages – including Tiani. He consoled himself knowing that this time he would be a mere mortal. The thought Prater might recognise him - even with fresh clothes and a shaven face - niggled at the back of his mind. Of course, when he reached home, he would have to get inside and that posed an entire new set of problems.

"Not sure I thought this through enough," he muttered as he stared at the trees before him.

Quinn made his own path as he descended the mountain. His thoughts turned to the immediate task of how long it would take to reach the bottom. Time pressed in on him knowing that as soon as Cecilia found the binding broken she would look to restart her plan.

"Ah, I probably should have put something in place. Maybe left Cashel a note. That probably would have been a great idea. A great idea unless he found it first, then I'd be listening to a lecture on all the reasons why it was a stupid thing to do..."

At first, his feet managed to avoid the roots from the trees and the petrified branches that lay on the ground, but then a stick decided he was in the way. He reached down and saw a small hole at the bottom of the pants. Quinn lifted it up as a pool of blood formed near his ankle. Healing had not been one of his magic skills. Some sorcerers could think about healing and it would happen, but Quinn had never managed to heal even the smallest of grazes. Cecilia had been no better from what he remembered. Only a handful of sorcerers were made into healers and most of them were useless at the rest of the magic.

Bending down, he pressed his thumb against the cut to try and stop the blood. He glanced back to the hole in his pants and winced. Unlike healing, Quinn had mastered mending of other materials including fabric and if he'd had his magic he could have fixed it - if he had his magic. He shook his head before moving his thumb.

"Oh, come on." The blood started to slowly leave the cut again. He yanked the cuff of the pants back down.

He looked up to see light still shining through the tree canopy. It felt like he'd been walking for hours, but he knew he had to keep moving until the darkness settled under the trees.

"Ah yes, darkness. That will be just what I need as well. The Academy really didn't prepare me for all this. Want to fix something - use magic. Want to start a fire - use magic. Want to do anything - use magic. Because magic is the great and wonderful difference that makes us better than humans,"

Quinn grumbled. He kicked a stone and watched as it disappeared into bushes to his side. "Humans might not have magic, but they make their houses with their hands, cook food, build a fire, and can fix a damn hole in their clothes."

He continued down the path until the trees blocked out any useful amount of light. With the darkness settled, Quinn sat down on a fallen tree trunk and pulled his aching foot closer. The blood had stopped, but streaks of dried blood trailed from the wound to his socks. He untied his boot and rolled his eyes.

"Clearly these boots weren't made for walking."

He eyed the holes in the sides and heel of the sock with contempt. Quinn contemplated removing the socks altogether but could see the way the sock clung to the back of his heel. He sighed into the night and stretched his leg back out to enjoy the coolness of the air as it passed around his foot. The moment of relief passed and he replaced his boot before he reached into his other boot to extract the small knife from within, relieved he'd thought to bring something. The blade fell into the grass beside him and he allowed his other foot to enjoy the coolness.

"Humans, it would seem, aren't as stupid as we're told."

He pulled his coat tighter around his body. His eyes watched for anything odd, but the shadows blended into the darkness. Quiet noises caused his gaze to dart from one place to another. Still, he knew that the loudest of the noises came from him. His stomach growled and he tried to ignore it as he slid onto the ground beside the trunk and curled himself in a ball. Despite his reservations about being attacked or eaten, sleep won out.

CHAPTER
TWENTY-TWO

Entering the village of Tiani, Quinn pulled his coat around him tightly, partially concealing his face. He had been walking the dirt roads that connected the villages, towns and cities for over a week and had the blistered feet to prove it. A farmer had provided Quinn with some relief and allowed him to travel in the rear of a cart, but they had parted ways in Haversy. While Quinn had been reluctant to stop, he rested the night under a tree as he had no money or goods to barter for a night indoors. A small stream had allowed him to clean himself of some of the dirt and grime, and a blade in his boot allowed him to keep any beard from appearing, though not without a learning curve.

He passed the burial yard as the mid-afternoon sun shone high above and noticed very few of the villagers about. Quinn had reminded himself not to gaze too long at the book building once he entered Tiani, but now it loomed beside him he paused, feeling compelled to look.

He stood on the street and stared through the open door. A few books were scattered on the ground, not destroyed, but ill-treated. Quinn felt a pang of guilt knowing his own actions made him partly responsible for the current state of the book building.

Quinn glanced around the street; the few people that were around weren't paying him any attention. He licked his lips before heading to the building and stepping inside of it. His eyes adjusted to the lighting as he lingered in the corridor before going into the main room. Piles of books around the room made it look both chaotic and organised. Some of those piles he knew Mary had made, but the room had many more than when she had called for him.

Perhaps someone went looking for something, Quinn turned, ready to walk closer to the closest pile. *Of course, that would mean someone other than Mary could read here otherwise there would be no point.*

Quinn felt sure the dragons were all too aware of the books. Even as he turned around to look at the half-filled shelves he couldn't escape the feeling the price to lift the binding might have been less had he not taken Mary away from the books.

He turned and left the room and felt the sun on his skin once more. Quinn turned to look up at the glass panel above the doorway, the dragon protecting the knowledge of the building within. *Time to go.*

"You there!"

Quinn froze, the familiar voice sent a chill down his spine. Prater.

"Yes, you there, with the long coat. Who are you?"

Prater stopped in front of Quinn. He looked Quinn up and down; his eyes seemed to study Quinn. Quinn reached his hands out slightly, in both a greeting and to steady himself. He swallowed hard as Prater's gaze remained on him.

"Quinn." For him it felt odd not adding anything additional about where he came from or even his title of that had to be used when in the presence of the Sorcery Council.

Quinn shifted his feet as he tried to ignore Prater as he circled him at a slow pace. His eyes focused ahead to the well until Prater came into view beside him. Memories of their last encounter nagged Quinn's mind. Prater came to a stop before him.

"You done? Can I go now?"

Prater smiled and resumed his course. With a sigh of frustration, Quinn did his best to avoid eye contact with Prater as he disappeared from view on his left before he reappeared on his right. After Quinn's last encounter with Prater, he had no desire to be put through the same ordeal again.

Quinn mentally shook his head to push the memory back and concentrate on the meeting before him.

"What's your business in this village?" Prater demanded.

"Nothing, I'm just passing through on my way home."

"Really?" Prater stepped close to Quinn. "Ever been here before?" Prater continued to circle him.

"No." He'd never wished to be as good at lying as his sister but wished now he'd paid more attention to how she made herself so convincing. Quinn hoped he sounded confident enough to foil any of the ideas Prater might have had revolving around his mind.

As Prater came to stand in front of him, Quinn saw Prater pull a piece of gold from a pocket in his long black coat. The gold sat neatly in the palm of his hand as he clutched it tight, watching Quinn.

"Are you a sorcerer?" Prater's eyes narrowed on Quinn.

"No."

"I don't like dragons but I spent a great deal of time trying to find a book. I don't like books either; they have the habit of giving people ideas that are best not thought of. Sometimes though, and this is rare, I do learn something new or in this case, corrected something I thought I knew."

"You would need to know how to read to learn something new from a book."

Prater's nose twitched. "We'll just skip that bit as it's not relevant to my point. You see I came across a book and I was bored so I opened it up. My father had told me that dragons and gold were a bad mix, that the gold could weaken their powers. Turns out, that was wrong. It turns out dragons aren't affected by gold at all and actually have a fondness for all things shiny. Sorcerers though, those that possess the conjuring magic, they're a different story. Did I mention I don't like sorcerers either? Anyway, apparently a sorcerer can be weakened by just touching gold and since I'm in search of one, I'm ensuring no one sneaks past me again."

"So what's your point? I don't read so none of this interests me much," Quinn replied.

"Take this in your hand."

Quinn balked at the sight of the gold. He knew the power the gold had to weaken his power and even take his life if it made contact for too long, but had no idea of what would happen now.

"Why?"

"Do you have some reason as to ask that?"

Quinn shrugged. Prater continued to look at Quinn as he resumed the walking the path he'd made in the dirt. "You don't look like a villager. Your clothes are not the browns and blacks that commoners wear, not even the well-off ones in the cities. Red, that's a bold colour to wear as a shirt, but that cloak, not many wear them anymore. Maybe you hesitate because you're a sorcerer?"

"I hesitate because I do not know why I should hold that stone."

"To prove that you aren't a sorcerer; you hold that piece of *stone* until the sun is at its highest in the day, and I shall let you pass through this village and be on your way."

"And if I refuse?"

That question brought a cynical smile and accompanying laugh from Prater. "Then I will hang you on principle."

Quinn knew that he had no choice but to touch the gold. He closed his eyes and wished himself a thousand kilometres away, which he could have done if he'd had his magic, before his eyes opened and he extended his hand to take the gold.

With the gold firmly grasped in his hand, Quinn felt no immediate change, except that his nerves were steadily increasing. The constant staring of Prater's evil eyes annoyed him; he was like an eagle watching for a mouse, ready to take flight in an instant to seize his prey. At length, Prater moved a little way off and barked an order for a chair to be brought to him by one of the children passing by. Dutifully the child returned with a chair.

"Why the test?" Quinn asked, looking over at Prater who looked comfortably relaxed on his chair.

"I'm searching for a young woman."

"That doesn't explain the gold."

Prater leaned forward and motioned his finger for Quinn to move closer. Walking towards him, Quinn turned the gold over in his hand. It seemed so innocent now, just a stone.

"Because, stranger, she could be in disguise."

"How could she be if she is a human?"

"Because stranger, there's sorcery involved in all this. I have a lot of trust issues and for very good reason.

"So who's this woman you are searching for?" Quinn queried. He knew Prater was referring to Mary, but the story sounded fantastical at best.

"Our book-keeper has been taken from us, and we want her to back."

"And these magical beings took her?"

"Well, I know someone did, not sure who, but it doesn't matter."

"If it doesn't matter, what then? Do you intend to go after both just because it will make you feel better?"

Prater got up from his chair closed the few steps to Quinn. The sun had some way still to rise before being at its zenith.

"Why are you so interested?" Prater paused. Around him the villagers continued with their work, as if there was nothing out of the ordinary seeing a man standing in the middle of the dirt divide holding a piece of rock in his hand.

"I have nothing else to think about while foolishly standing here, plus, it sounds like an interesting story."

"An interesting story?" Prater turned his attention to the broken door of the book building. "I'll tell you an interesting story. There was this girl, a quiet girl who steered clear of everyone else in the village. With her family all dead, she was taken in by the local book-keeper. She learnt to read and write and take care of the books – which she continued to do after the book-keeper passed. Then though, she read one book, and this one book gave her ideas and she freed a man from the cells who was to be hung. She disappeared and then came back again. Another man disappeared from the cell, and I find out this girl has been bound to another, but he isn't around. All the pieces fall together then. I was too blind to see that she was the one freeing the men, but then she disappears from inside a room and this time she doesn't return."

"And now you are trying to find her," Quinn added, finishing the story that had a familiar ring to it.

"Exactly." Prater started back to his chair.

"So why do you want to find her?" Quinn felt the words may make him sound too involved or invested in the story, so he added, "Since she obviously worked behind your back to free these men?"

"Because her place is here."

"You're going to hang her?"

A conceited smile crossed over Prater's smug face. "No, I want to be bound to her."

The comment caught Quinn by surprise; he had thought the man beyond feelings for anyone but himself, and Mary had not given him any indication of feelings for Prater. Quinn reasoned that with Prater probably didn't care for Mary, but only with possessing something at a particular moment in time he wanted.

"Look around, you see many girls here? I've known her all my life and we have certain things in common, like reading. As much as I despise the skill it isn't as worthless as I thought once." Prater looked past Quinn. "And returning Mary to keep the books might just bring me some of that dragon luck."

"Then shouldn't you be looking for the man she is bound to?" The smug look vanished from Prater's face.

"That's a very good idea. Get me a horse, Delwyn," Prater yelled at a young man, who hurried off to fulfil the demand. Prater turned his attention back to the Quinn. Quinn's hand ached from holding the gold but that was it. "And you, you can come with me."

Quinn breathed with relief at the prospect of not standing any longer. The gold had not affected him in the slightest but still, as he held it in his hand, a wariness of it remained. Turning his thoughts to Mary, he wondered if the binding record would exist since he had broken it.

But it did still take place, Quinn thought to himself on the subject, *so it should be there. And with the binding broken it won't be long before Cecilia finds out, she's not stupid. And once she knows she'll go back to Michael. If Prater finds them, it will lead right back to me.*

Two horses trotted towards Quinn led by Delwyn. Prater tapped Quinn on the shoulder and took the gold from his hand, hiding it back away into his pocket. Prater nodded at the dappled brown and cream mare and then looked to Quinn. Stepping towards the horse, it turned its head and watched him with dark eyes; Quinn hadn't been on a horse since the Academy – and that experience had been just another he would have preferred to forget about.

Casting his eyes to the side, Quinn saw Prater mount his own cream mare. With a formal pose, he glanced around the village before his eyes found Quinn again.

"You need a special invitation? I'm assuming you can ride, otherwise you're about to get a very intense lesson."

Quinn inwardly snarled at Prater but after patting the horse on the neck, hooked his foot into the stirrup and threw his leg over. He could cope easily with moving through space with magic but the feeling of being so high off the ground made his stomach turn and his eyes blur. His parents had taught him to ride; they had valued creatures and Cecilia had been insistent to learn, determined that when she was older she'd find a unicorn or pegasus of her own. Focusing on the mare's head, Quinn picked up the worn rein and tugged on one side so she turned around.

CHAPTER
TWENTY-THREE

In a cloud of dust, the two riders entered Haversy. After orientating himself, Prater turned the horse towards the left road and Quinn nodded in response, following Prater's cloudy trail until they reached a large building. Quinn had always thought the gathering building could use a bit of style since all the ones he'd seen were identical. *Still, it makes them easy to find.*

Quinn pulled on the reins and his mare slowed down until she trotted up to her horse companion and stopped. Prater had already dismounted and headed up the stairs two at a time. Turning his head, Quinn thought about seizing the moment and taking off on the horse, but he tucked the idea away and dismounted, catching his shoe in the stirrup as he did. Landing on the ground, the horse turned towards him.

"Yeah, very funny, I'm here for your amusement." The horse whinnied in response before seeking out the lush grass at her hooves.

Standing up, Quinn's back ached, his backside a combination of pins and needles and numbness. He raised his eyes in time to see Prater disappear through the door. He gave the horse another reassuring pat on the side before waddling towards the stairs hoping his body would return to feeling normal quickly.

"Binding man!" Prater's voice demanded as the double wooden doors exploded open as he entered the main room from the entrance in a fury. Ahead, a wide-eyed man stood clutching a book in his arms with his mouth hanging open. "Binding man, I need information."

"Please," Quinn muttered as he walked into the room.

The man raised his eyebrows and smiled, though Quinn thought it resembled the way he looked when he'd had to greet a distant relative who insisted on tight hugs and covering him with kisses. Quinn casually followed Prater, and as he approached the binding man, he brushed the dirt from his clothes.

Despite having seen many gathering rooms from the outside, Quinn had never been inside one. Following behind Prater, he noticed it differed from what he had imagined, far less ornate and without the huge bouquets of flowers everywhere. He'd never given much thought to the ceremony; being bound had always been something humans did. Still, his thoughts wandered to what Mary's ceremony to Michael might have been like, what Cecilia's would be to Michael if he didn't find another way to stop her plan once she kick-started it again. A sorcerer would only need a gathering room if they were being bound to a human and being against the rules…Quinn, had watched a few partnership contracts signed at the Sorcery Council's offices, not their private levels, just the general admittance one. He'd never be able to go there again without his powers. Choosing a partner had predominately been a decision made by the Council. Quinn resented the Council for many things, including how hard it had been for him to hold onto friendships from school, let alone entertaining any other thoughts beyond friendship.

"I need to know about a man and woman who were bound here, not so long ago."

The man stepped over to the large book that sat on the podium and glanced up at Prater. "My son,

I will need more information to go by if I am to find them in the records."

"Her name was Mary, she was from Tiani. The man – I don't know his name."

"Ah yes, I remember them," the binding man chuckled and turned a few pages back in search of the record and then added, "She seemed a lot keener than he to be bound."

"What is his name?" Prater's demanded. His foot tapped against the stone floor at a furious pace.

"Michael, Michael of Yevma." Quinn's ears pricked at the familiar district name. Cecilia had set up a home in that district, choosing a human home over the magical style that Quinn had. He had been there a few times in search of his sister but had not known that Michael lived so close. "Hmm, that's strange..."

"What's strange?" Prater demanded and stepped forward, pushing the man slightly to the side as he looked at the book.

"The record number has been stricken through, odd – they both seemed so healthy and young – one of them might have died – the binding is broken."

Quinn closed his eyes and thanked the dragon; any small doubt that might have remained about him keeping his word vanished. Still, as he watched a pensive Prater at the podium, he wondered what would happen now. With Mary free of the binding it meant Quinn now had the other issue of ensuring Mary didn't get bound to someone she didn't want to.

"Is there any way of knowing for sure what broke the binding?" Prater asked cautiously.

The man tapped his fingers against the book he held, "According to folklore there are supposed to be many ways of breaking a binding besides death – but I couldn't say..."

"Are you sure there is no way of finding out?" Prater looked at the binding man, whose face clouded over as he straightened himself up.

"I have already told you that..."

"But I need to know!"

"These records maintain themselves, sir. You'll need to either find where they went or go find a dragon and ask them since all this is their forte in action. *I* can't assist you further." The man turned and left with hurried footsteps, and Quinn suppressed laughter at the indignation the man displayed.

Prater looked up at Quinn, and he tried to cover his smile with a discrete cough.

"Your suggestion was helpful, maybe strangers aren't all so bad." Quinn didn't like the sound of that; he wanted to return home and the physical entrance was still a distance away. "I could use a man like you around. We'll head back to Tiani to fetch more men."

"I didn't say I would help you."

Prater looked over at him. "Help me this once and that horse is yours."

Riding on a horse will be much quicker than walking, Quinn nodded in agreement. *A few more days away from Cashel isn't going to make much of a difference anyway.*

****

Riding into the village, Quinn noticed Delwyn running towards Prater as he waved a piece of paper in his hand.

"You got a response, Master. The rider came from Riejan."

"I hoped pestering the book building caretakers might lead to something. Let's see if it's good news." Prater dismounted, almost falling in his haste as the heel of his boot caught in the stirrup before he reached his hand out. "Come here, Delwyn. Let me read it!"

Prater snatched the letter. Delwyn took a step backward and clasped his hands behind his back as he lowered his head. Quinn spurred his horse forward trying to see what information the paper contained. Prater glanced up as Quinn circled from behind. Quinn dismounted and joined Prater's side.

"It's a letter from some man called Elkan from the sea city of Riejan. He says, well, I'll just read it. 'A young lady is my newest student. Her name is Mary and comes from some way away, though she will not say from where. She is bound to Michael of Yevma of the manor on the hill. You will remember I told you of the mysteriousness surrounding his return some time ago with a binding mark, yet no wife. She is a very keen student to teach, and I am surprised at how quickly she is working through her lessons. I wonder as to whether she has been taught to read before as she makes connections with letters and sounds without much instruction. In regards to Michael though, it is a strange thing indeed. I believe I wrote to you when he was to be bound to a beautiful woman called Cecilia. She though hasn't been seen since Michael returned here. There are some who believe she isn't as she seems...'"

Turning to Delwyn, Prater asked, "Where's the city of Riejan? It must be close to this Yevma manor."

"Riejan is right on the outskirts of the Great Forest to the west."

"Send out a messenger to direct the men to Riejan and gather as many men as you can from the village…we're going to sort this sorcerer and human mess out, once and for all."

Quinn followed Prater to his house to relax and enjoy something to eat before heading for Riejan. The thought of heading through the Great Forest to where he'd contacted the dragon caused him to shift uncomfortably in the chair as he stared at the fire before him. He'd been eager to make contact with Cashel again, but it seemed a bigger plan needed to unfold first.

Prater placed a tray of food on the table between the chairs and sat down himself. He didn't hesitate to begin eating the meal.

"What did you mean about the sorcerer?" Quinn asked after devouring the last morsel from his plate.

Prater looked over as he set his own empty plate on the little table. He leaned back, stretched his arms out, and rested behind his head.

"This Michael, he's caused a few problems and I need to ensure one has been resolved. I told you about Mary before, and now we both know that she is, well was, bound to him. Well, he was the reason a sorceress, Cecilia, came to the village. Gorgeous thing, but dangerous – all sorcerers are, you know? Mary claimed to be bound to a mortal, but I can't understand why would someone protect a mortal? I don't know, maybe he is a sorcerer and she lied. Either way, we'll find out."

"So, you are going after him for what then?" Quinn asked.

"I might just hang him from the nearest tree on principle."

"Surely he must be dead as the binding is broken."

"Nothing is ever that simple in life. I have the feeling that both are still alive. If I am correct about that then this Michael is still alive, but he won't be for much longer if I find he's a sorcerer."

"You hate sorcerers as much as dragons then?"

"I hate anything that dares to cross the kingdom boundaries. There was a good reason for each to be separated."

Quinn squirmed again in his chair. He crossed, before uncrossing, his legs. "Do you hope to win Mary's heart?"

Prater sneered and shrugged his shoulders. "You can't force something that isn't there, but I'm confident I'll prevail in what I want."

CHAPTER
TWENTY-FOUR

The carriage pulled up in front of the book building in Riejan. Michael and Mary sat in uncomfortable silence. Neither had talked about the broken binding – they had both noticed, and a look between them had decided that things would need to change. Mary had wondered how Michael might have broken it when she hadn't seen him gone from the manor for more than a day at most. She had considered the alternative as well, that it hadn't been Michael at all, and that Quinn might have. That thought had been discarded quickly as she reminded herself that breaking the binding would only complicate Quinn's own situation.

"You don't have to leave, Mary. Mother likes having you around," Michael said and turned his head to look at her. She held her bag tightly with her possessions safely packed inside.

"I stayed nearly a week after the binding broke, and that was probably longer than I should," Mary replied. Michael nodded and shifted his feet. "I am sorry, for everything. I am sure we won't cross paths again. I wish you well, Michael."

"I guess despite it all I'm lucky Cecilia has forgiven me getting bound to you."

"You've heard from her?" Mary asked, surprised.

Michael nodded. "She came to see me away from the house. My binding to her is back on. I don't know that I can forgive you Mary, but I guess there's more to what happened than I know. A bit of advice though: don't do it to another man. You should be with someone because you care for them."

Mary glanced at the ground. It was hard to hear his rebuke, but she knew he had a point. She hoped that somehow maybe she might get a second chance too.

"Good luck, Michael."

Michael stared beyond Mary. She had thought he would say something in reply, but by the time she had awkwardly dismounted the carriage and managed not to drop her bag, he continued to sit in the same silence.

Standing on the pavement, she felt comforted that she would soon be back in the familiarity of a book building. Elkan had been surprised when she had turned up the previous day. The excitement for the binding mark vanishing had given her the energy to walk the distance into the town to see him. Mary had told him of the news in awe, only for him to sit back in his chair, his fingers tapping on the arm of his chair while his eyes gazed at the bookshelf off to one side.

Mary felt that she should say something more, perhaps even apologise again, but no more words wanted to be spoken. After she stepped back, away from the carriage, Michael flicked the reins and continued down the street. Mary felt disappointed that he hadn't said anything in return, didn't explain the broken binding, and didn't turn back.

Mary watched the carriage until it disappeared from view. She glanced down, drawn to the bare white skin of her hand that no longer had a black ink marking. In her heart she knew she still wanted the chance to see Quinn again. She wished that she hadn't left the stone behind but reminded herself that he was still a sorcerer. She turned and ascended the stairs to her new home.

****

The days passed differently in the book building. At the manor, days had felt drawn out and stilted, but surrounded by books again, and learning the words to read them again, the days passed by with something new to see and learn.

Still, whenever she looked at her hand, it reminded her that there were many things in the kingdom she didn't know about. One night, as the fire burned brightly, she decided to see if Elkan knew anything more, or could at least point her in the direction of where she might find out.

"Elkan?"

Aged eyes looked up from the pages of the book he was reading and focused on Mary. "Yes child?"

"I know about the Golden Law and all that, but what about the history of the three kingdoms. I've never really thought about it much before, things were just how they are. It's not that I don't know anything at all, but I wonder about the dragon kingdom and the sorcerer one."

"Well, if you think I am that old, child, then I hate to disappoint you. The boundaries between the dragon and human kingdoms blurred some time back, though sorcerers have always kept to themselves."

"But dragons rarely have anything to do with humans either, do they? Because of the rules that are in place."

"I'm afraid you may know more about the topic than I do. Dragons maintain the records, the books around us, but each one was written by a human. I'm not sure if the magic they put on the books was some kind of recompense for the war that occurred with the sorcerers or not. If it was, then I would be very interested to know what sort of compensation the sorcerers made to the humans."

"Humans got caught in the middle?"

"Very much so. I don't know what started the war between the two kingdoms, but I do know that many humans lost their lives in the crossfire, innocent people. A treaty was made between the two sides but how that came about I don't know."

"How can there be so much about our own history we don't know? I mean, what happened back then impacts what people have been taught to believe generation after generation and yet none of us really seem to fully understand what even happened."

"I know the three kingdoms lived peacefully while they lived separately. Dragons can shift into human form; did you know that?" Elkan asked.

"Yes, I did."

"I remember years ago when I was chatting with a dear friend," he pulled out a cord from which a yellow stone hung, "he said that dragons no longer have that power. He believed that the dragons that remain can no longer shift into a human form at all."

"A consequence of the Great War?"

Elkan shrugged and leaned forward to prod the fire with the poker, before he settled back into his chair. "That I don't know. Dragons crossed into the human kingdom and some chose to live as humans. From what I've heard that happened over a long period of time, though it wasn't really talked about, but people knew. Then the Great War happened, and each kind was to keep to their own once again."

"It kind of seems strange to try and reverse something that had already happened."

"It was more likely damage control. I believe some dragons returned to their kingdom, but a great number continue to live in the Great Forest. There must have been some reason they moved from their territory in the first place, but I don't believe I've read a single book on the subject."

"The dragons said their land was dying and that they had no choice."

"And who told you that?"

Mary smiled; she'd told Elkan a little of what had happened but knew she'd left out quite a bit on purpose. "A sorcerer. He told me a little of what he knew."

"A sorcerer? You've spoken of this sorceress with the fiery temper but not a sorcerer. Child, you have met more magical beings in your very short life than I have in my very long life. And what else did this sorcerer say?"

Mary looked at her lap as she recalled the night Quinn had told her about the Great War. "Quinn, I mean, the sorcerer, he said that they didn't know if the dragons were telling the truth about the land dying. Both sides though accused the other of things and eventually they battled in hopes of one side having more power than the other."

"I don't know about that but I guess that anything is indeed possible. The problem is that exceptions run rampant through rules that have been carefully crafted. From what I've read dragon and sorcerer magic doesn't work the same way;

both sides have magic but both are able to counter the others' magic. It wouldn't make much sense then for the sides to start something as devastating as the Great War. It would be like watching two snakes trying to kill each other with venom that they were both immune to."

"I believe they found a way around that, a way to tip the magic balance in their favour."

"The dragons or the sorcerers?"

"Both, but I suspect they'd probably blame the other side for being the first to do so."

"And how did they accomplish such a thing?" Elkan leaned forward.

"Humans were apparently the key, still are the key, sort of."

"Human, huh? Us with no magic are the most powerful of all?" Elkan chuckled.

"I always believed that all dragons were good, but they're not, are they?"

"No, just like not all sorcerers are good and not all mortals are good. I sometimes wonder that perhaps the world needs a certain balance of good and bad to survive."

Silence settled and Mary fidgeted with her dress. Elkan had been kind enough to provide her with shelter and hadn't asked for an explanation, even after the binding mark had finished. She assumed he'd noticed; she'd assumed he would be curious, and yet he never pressed the subject. Mary though knew she trusted him as much as she had Yansa.

"I read something, Elkan; I thought it would bring me good luck – dragon luck."

"Eh? It sounds like you did more than read something; you did something about what you read, didn't you, child?" Elkan turned in his chair.

Mary's gaze met with Elkan's and she averted her eyes as they misted over.

"You worry about the man you care for?"

"Michael is fine…" Mary started.

"That is not what I asked, Mary." Elkan reached out placed his hand gently on Mary's knee. "It sounds to me that this other man cared for you too."

"But that doesn't matter, does it, Elkan? Each of the three kingdoms was meant to remain separate. That's what the Golden Law says and Quinn is a sorcerer. Even if the binding has somehow been broken I am still a human and he isn't."

Elkan withdrew his hand and sat back in the chair, sinking into the fabric.

"Sometimes it is best to just wait and see what your future will bring rather than worrying about things that may never happen. The binding is broken, and I'm sure an explanation of how that happened will be revealed in its own time and way."

CHAPTER
TWENTY-FIVE

The fire burned low and hot; there was no wind to disrupt the constant, chaotic rhythm of the flames. Two days, it had only been two days since the group has left Haversy, but for Quinn it had been a *long* two days. Quinn had settled to rest feeling rather comfortable, or as comfortable as someone could be sitting on hard, dry ground leaning against a tree three times his own diameter with bark peeled away in long coarse strips. Quinn wondered if it was those strips of bark, that hung from various spots on the tree, which were making his skin crawl each time he brushed against a piece. He shivered at the thought of what secrets, or creatures, those strips of bark kept hidden.

The cloudless night was providing more than enough light to see, though the fire hid much of the surroundings that were out of its reach. From his position against the tree, Quinn studied Prater.

For the better part of the journey to Riejan, they had not spoken – at least Quinn hadn't. Occasionally Prater had interrupted the monotony of riding to offer unsolicited advice and thoughts on anything he felt like. Quinn watched as Prater kicked out his foot to prop himself up against the tree.

"You don't like to talk about yourself, do you? All these days and I'm none the wiser about you or where you're from. Is there no one waiting for you?" Prater's words were casual as he pulled a knife from his boot and started cutting a stick.

"Just an empty house," Quinn replied but felt guilty omitting Cashel.

"You're not eager to return home?"

"I'm in no hurry."

Prater leant forward. "You follow me for a horse. Why would you have travelled so far without one to begin with?"

Quinn broke eye-contact and linked his fingers together behind his head. He focused on the stars twinkling in the night sky over head.

"I didn't think it through."

"You don't come across as being a stupid man."

Quinn smiled, "Neither do you, and yet you are pursuing a man clear across this land for the purpose of…"

"At first revenge, to save face, but now, now it is just answers," Prater paused. He leaned back and rubbed his jaw. "…and revenge as well."

"Revenge doesn't accomplish anything."

"Speaking from experience?"

Quinn looked over at Prater. "You don't always learn from your own experience – sometimes seeing what other people do and go through are enough."

"Perhaps that's why you are returning to an empty house. You really have no other family?"

Quinn hesitated before replying, "I have family."

"Must be nice having a family. It's been a long time since I had one. When I look around Tiani it's like a constant reminder that families ceased to exist for us years ago."

"I saw many families." Quinn glanced over to Prater in time to see the creases form on his forehead.

"You saw the remains of families. Empty shells that once were families. It's never been like it was before."

"A family isn't always just parents and children. It can be strangers with a common purpose, a community – family is a sense, a feeling – not a thing."

"An interesting idea, but family is the flesh and blood that is formed from one generation to another. No bond will ever be stronger than blood."

"Not even love?"

Prater laughed. "If I ever had to choose between love and blood, I know which would win every time."

Quinn watched Prater shake his head before closing his eyes. The spoken conversation had ended but what Prater said continued to turn over in Quinn's mind. He'd never separated thoughts of love and blood; Cashel and Cecilia were equal to him as family, yet he wondered who he would choose if he had to. The feeling unsettled him as the answer evaded him even as he drifted off to sleep.

****

Three days of travelling passed without incident until on the fourth day, Prater's horse kicked a shoe. A small village a short distance away provided Quinn and Prater with the chance to pause. Quinn surveyed the village. It might have been the same size as some of the villages around Tiani but it wasn't the same. As he looked around Quinn could see smiling faces of people, children everywhere and strange inventions and things – like children running along while something flew in the air.

"It won't be ready until tomorrow," the blacksmith informed Prater after looking at the horse's hoof.

"Why such a wait?" Prater replied impatiently.

The middle-aged blacksmith smiled, showing slightly yellowed teeth beneath his red moustache.

"Young man I believe that everyone must wait their turn for what they want, others are before you so you must wait."

"But I'm in a hurry."

Quinn shifted in his own saddle before dismounting. His feet were pleased to be back on the ground but his legs felt stiff from the long stretches of riding. He watched as Prater paced back and forth in front of the blacksmith whose face didn't falter even when Quinn saw him look his way.

"There has to be some way to expedite this matter; name your price."

"Boy, I value all my customers, and I demonstrate that by doing them in order of when they come to me. Unless it's a matter of life and death. Impatience is not a matter of life and death in my humble opinion, so if you're in such a hurry you're welcome to reshoe the horse yourself. After all, it would also cost you less."

"Fine," grumbled Prater and the blacksmith whistled. A young boy appeared and took the rein from Prater's hand.

Prater walked back towards Quinn. "All good then?"

"I want you to ride ahead to Riejan; I need to try and counter this delay somehow." Prater patted the horse as it drank from the water trough before he turned back to Quinn and pulled him aside. "We've bonded the past few days, but don't think you can just ride off with my horse without keeping your end of the deal. I know your name and will track you down. I'll wait here for the remaining men and I'll catch up in a day or so."

"And what is it you want me to do in Riejan?" Quinn felt Prater's hand connect hard with the back of his head. "Ow! What was that for?"

"What do you think you should do? Find out where the manor is. Find out any information about this Michael, I suspect there's a wedding being organised to take place as we head there. I need to make sure Mary stays put at the book building in the city until I finish the other business I have."

"Right."

Quinn whistled and rubbed the back of his head as his horse turned away from the water and trotted over to him. Quinn nodded once more to Prater before he mounted the horse. His legs immediately objected to the familiar position, but he hoped to find somewhere sheltered they could both properly rest for the night. Clicking his tongue, Quinn flicked the rein to urge the horse on. He headed down the road in the direction of Riejan. He wished he would find Mary at the book building and hoped that his task could somehow be resolved without any more consequences.

The thundering of the horse's hooves on the hard-packed earth announced Quinn's presence on the road. He hoped the opportunity to be there first might slow down Prater's plan at least. Quinn had passed by Michael's home, but the thought that Mary might have chosen to go to Michael was something he hadn't anticipated.

As the night drew around Quinn, he had little choice but to stop. Allowing his horse to rest and graze nearby, Quinn lay down on the dry grass and stared up at the darkness. He wondered at the simple scene of a dark sky scattered with diamonds as he knew it was all far more complex than that.

Closing his eyes, Quinn felt tired, but his mind continued to turn over everything from the past few weeks – his life as a sorcerer seemed far in the past. His mouth curled into a half-smile at the thought of the past and the future that he felt he could reach out and touch.

CHAPTER
TWENTY-SIX

"Can I assist you?"

Quinn dismounted his horse and walked up the steps two at a time to where the old man stood unlocking the door.

"Mary; is Mary here?" he said while attempting to catch his breath.

"Why yes, she's inside, and who might you…" but Quinn was already heading past the man and into the book building.

Quinn's eyes took a moment to adjust to the dimmer light inside. He leaned through the nearest doorway but found only empty chairs and books scattered on the table. Turning, he headed across the hall to another room and again looked inside. He hit his hand against the frame in frustration before he headed further down the hall.

"Young man, if you would…"

The words faded behind him as Quinn looked into another room. He turned to leave before shifting his feet back and taking another look. Mary sat at the end of the table with a book in her hands staring in his direction.

"Mary."

"Quinn, I thought I heard your voice but then I wasn't sure because...well, why would you be here in Riejan of all places?"

Quinn's feet shuffled for a moment before he crossed the room to her. He took the book from her hands and placed it on the table. "We need to leave here, Mary. I don't think Prater will be far behind me."

"Prater is coming? Why would he be coming here?"

Mary glanced down at her hand as she stood up at the able. "The binding mark is gone; it just vanished one night while I was asleep."

Quinn reached out to hold her hand. "I know, the binding is broken. Come on, we need to get you out of here."

"And go where?"

Quinn hesitated; he hadn't thought beyond reaching her first. "I don't know; just not here."

"I don't think Prater is coming here for me, Quinn." Mary looked up at Quinn's face. "And anyway, even if he was coming here for some reason, I can't keep running forever from one place to the next. This might be the place I'm staying at the moment, Quinn, but I do want to return to my home at some point."

"I can respect all that, but Mary, there is a time and place to make your stand and now isn't it."

"Has this got something to do with Cecilia?"

"Yes, it does. Come on, I can explain in more detail later, but for now can we just get out of here?"

"Would someone care to fill me in on what's going on? Young man, perhaps start by introducing yourself?" Elkan's loud, assertive voice echoed through the room and both turned to see him standing in the doorway.

"Quinn..."

"Ah, the sorcerer I have heard about."

Quinn turned to look at Mary with eyebrows raised. He hadn't expected her to have shared anything. The unexpected feeling inside him returned and a smile crossed his face.

"You told him about me?

"I did."

"I, young man, am Elkan and this is my book building that you are in and so I would like to know what is going on."

His hand gave hers a squeeze before he turned back to Elkan who had moved closer to the pair.

"I'm Quinn, but I'm not a sorcerer, not anymore at least. I need to get Mary away somehow for a while, just to keep her safe while everything else plays out."

"It's safe here."

"Not safe enough. There's a lot going on, and I know you mean well, but I'd feel better knowing Mary was somewhere else where Prater won't know to look."

"Give me a few moments to gather some things; rushing out in haste will make you prone to making foolish mistakes. I think I have a plan." Elkan turned and started shuffling back towards the doorway. "Ah, reminds me of the mysterious adventures I had as a youth with my own sorcerer friend."

The old man disappeared before the words registered with Quinn and he could open his mouth to ask further about the childhood friend. Still,

Quinn knew that there were more important matters that needed to be dealt with first.

"It was you who broke the binding, wasn't it?" Mary asked.

Quinn continued to hold her hand in his and closed his eyes, allowing his forehead to touch Mary's; with his free hand his index finger lightly touched Mary's lips. "I promised you I would do whatever I could."

"But you didn't give up..." Mary's voice faltered. "You gave up your magic, didn't you? That's why you said...Why would you do that Quinn? Breaking the binding wasn't worth losing your powers."

"I made you a promise to have it broken, and maybe this is my way of trying to find a bit of that good luck that you've been trying to find yourself."

"But Quinn, without your magic...That was part of your life."

"Well maybe it's time to start a new chapter in my life, too. First though, I have to at least try to do something to stop my sister in the morning, that's when they're being bound isn't it?"

"Yes, at the main gathering room up on the hill. There's been talk of it for days. What do you think you can do?"

"Wish for some dragon luck?"

"Okay, I have here some supplies for you to take with you. It's not a lot but I get the sense this is only a short-term arrangement anyway," Elkan said as he entered the room carrying a bag in one hand. "There are some old castle ruins, I believe they once belonged to a sorcerer - though I'm not that old. Still, one day I should catch up with Cashel and ask him more about that."

Quinn took the offered bag with his free hand. "You know Cashel?"

"Why, yes, I do, though it has been a long while since I saw him. He got busy with duties at the Sorcery Academy and I found my own place here to keep me busy. You know him too?"

"Yeah, we're close."

"Have you consulted him on your plan?"

"I have no way of contacting him any longer."

"Well, we have time to get him here."

"We really should go..."

"I know you think everything needs to be done this second, young man, but I assure you we have the time. Sometimes taking things a bit slower allows for the mind to be clearer."

Elkan reached under his top and pulled out a yellow stone that hung from the leather cord. He smiled as he gave it a rub. Quinn recognised the stone; he'd had a similar one to summon Cashel when he first got his assignment, before he could control his magic fully.

A spray of warm yellow sparkles spun around before a shape appeared in the centre. Quinn retreated a little at seeing the back of his mentor; he'd hoped to not have any discussion about his deal with Jharobi quite so soon.

"Elkan, my friend! It has been too long!" The two men embraced before Elkan nodded towards Quinn and Mary.

Cashel turned around and his features melted from a smile to a frown. "Quinn and Mary, what's going on here? Don't tell me you…"

"I did what I felt was right, Cashel; you can tell me off later. Right now, I need to get Mary out of here and stop Cecilia's binding." Quinn tried to make it sound as practical an idea as he could.

"We will talk later." Cashel's stare proved too much for Quinn and he looked at the floor. "When is the binding?"

"Tomorrow," Elkan replied. "But we have a plan that they would be safe for a few days at the old ruins. Quinn wants Mary somewhere safe until he completes what he has come here to do.”

“What's it all got to do with her? If the binding is broken…What do I not know? Quickly, we haven't got all afternoon,” Cashel said.

“Prater is headed here as well; he's after everyone, Michael, Cecilia, and Mary,” Quinn said..

“Quinn, this is why it is simpler for humans and sorcerers to stay out of each other's business, but I suppose you'll tell me it's Cecilia's fault for starting it all?” Cashel rubbed his eyes.

“Not going to argue there,” Quinn mumbled.

“Cashel, would you stay here, I recall discussions when weren't so grey about a book of predictions,” Elkan suggested.

“I remember you bringing it up, vaguely. Before anything else though, we need to have a quick discussion about something,” Cashel said. “Where are you going then?”

“I'll take them to the ruins. Perhaps one day you'll fill in Quinn about its history, but not today.” Elkan said as he turned to walk out of the room. “Come on you two, we will get moving. Now where is that horse I can borrow…”

“Go ahead Mary: I'll be there in a moment,” Quinn said.

Mary nodded and Quinn let go of her hand, taking the bag from him, and followed Elkan's pathway out of the door and towards the entrance.

"Cashel..." Quinn started to say.

"You can't change what you've done, Quinn. My only hope is that you can complete your assignment from the Council. You know, it won't matter to them that you've traded away your magic," Cashel said.

"I was more worried about you being angry with me than the Council."

"I'm not over the moon, but who am I to judge in the end. You're a grown man, Quinn, it's time I let you make decisions and accept whatever consequences appear as a result. Go on, let's see what happens."

Quinn nodded and walked towards Cashel. He wanted to give him a hug, but the old man simply smiled and continued past him.

"Quinn, good luck son," Cashel said.

Quinn lingered in the doorway for a moment; his teeth pressed against his lip. He didn't look back, but instead turned towards the entrance of the book building in time to see Elkan mounting a horse with extreme ease considering how slowly he walked.

By the time he reached the main door he saw Mary had hold the reins of the horse he'd ridden there. He cupped his hands to help push her up towards the saddle before settling in behind her.

"Follow me!" Elkan flicked the reins and the horse trotted around them before building up to a canter. By the time they'd all navigated their way through the streets their pace had quickened. Once they reached the edge of the city where tracks diverted away from the main road they were galloping.

Trees passed them by on both sides as they rode through the outer portion of the Great Forest. Quinn wasn't quite sure what to expect but after a bit he saw rocks scattered beside the path they were on. Then, amongst the trees, the ruins of a castle appeared. Quinn pulled up hard on the reins as Mary grabbed part of the horse's mane.

The horse slowed to a trot and before coming to a stop, Quinn dismounted and cast his eyes over the castle. The castle wasn't just run down and forgotten; whatever the castle had witnessed in the past had destroyed most of it. Quinn turned back to Mary and he reached up to help her down. He held her around her waist for a moment longer than he would have before.

Mary wandered towards the castle as Quinn busied himself unsaddling the horse and removing the bridle, turning the horse away to allow it to graze at its leisure.

Elkan waited near the crumbled steps that lead to what Quinn thought had once been the entrance. A door hung open at an angle battling with a vine to stay upright. The windows no longer had any glass, and more than a few birds had decided that the broken walls that loomed over them were the perfect nesting locations. Despite the way it looked, they were surrounded by silence, and with that silence, Quinn felt a sense of relief and safety.

"Stay here for the night at least. There should be a spring of fresh water in one of the rooms towards the centre," Eklan instructed.

"Where is the gathering room from here?" Quinn asked.

"Back down the way we come but take the first paved road to your right. Follow it and you'll find yourself taken directly there."

"Thank you." Quinn nodded to Elkan.

"Thank me when all this is resolved." Elkan walked back down the steps and paused beside Quinn. The old man grabbed Quinn's hand and placed a pouch in his hand before folding Quinn's fingers over it. "Cashel wanted you to have this."

Quinn looked at his hand but didn't look inside the pouch. He placed it inside the pocket of his pants knowing whatever it contained could wait until later.

CHAPTER
TWENTY-SEVEN

"I guess we have some time to explore before the sun sets. It's not much to fix up," Mary said as she looked up towards the top of the broken walls.

"No, just needs a little work."

Mary smiled at Quinn's understatement. "Not much for a sorcerer to fix."

Quinn smiled. "Pity it is much more for a man to fix."

"Is there a chance you could get your magic back?"

"No, I don't think so."

Mary smiled over at him, intending for it to be comforting. She had questions though. If Prater intended to come to Riejan then there had to be a good reason.

"I can almost read again. Elkan's been working with me every day. There are still some times that I have to work out a word, but it is getting easier." Mary stepped through the doorway and looked around at the crumbled walls. A large fountain sat towards the back of the large open room with water still trickling over the sides. "Elkan has been telling me about schools."

"Schools?"

Mary's smile widened. "Elkan told me that the books say that long ago children would go to school every day to learn how to read and write. They'd learn about the land and the weather and about everything around us," Mary paused, and Quinn waited, watching her. "I'm going back to Tiani, Quinn. Tiani is my home. It's the only place I've ever known, and I want to go back there – to teach the children."

"But there are no children in Tiani, and Prater…"

"There are children in the other villages around us, and the curse that happened…that took away the children, maybe it needs us to stop living like we all froze in time. I think we're all too scared to move on from what happened, to accept that there's nothing we can change about that. Running away to another village isn't going to help me accept that and deal with it, and the book building there…I think I could make it into a real home and a school."

"But Prater…"

"I don't care about Prater or his plans or whatever he thinks is going to happen." Mary paused and sat on the edge of the stone that contained the water that trickled from the top of the fountain. "Quinn, I lived my life in hope that *something* would change it. I've learnt to read twice now and that's taught me something: I need to be the one to change. I can't just keep wishing or hoping or waiting on anyone else."

"It wouldn't be safe though, Mary…Prater…he…he has a plan…which includes you…" Quinn said and sat down beside Mary. His fingers trailed over the water's surface.

Mary rested her hand on Quinn's; she saw his hand curl into a ball so tightly that the knuckles begun to turn white. She smiled and tried to connect with his gaze.

"Quinn…Quinn, look at me." Quinn sighed and raised his eyes and looked at her. "You've given up a lot…but maybe…I mean if you wanted to…"

"I have to stop my sister."

"But after that   Quinn. You haven't told me everything I'm sure, but maybe this isn't just my chance to break free from the past - maybe it's time you did the same thing."

"When I was told I had to be my sister's keeper, make sure she stayed away from humans, make sure that she didn't go near the Golden Law... I accepted that it wasn't something I could refuse. I think I was too young to realise just what they were asking of me."

"What's the worst that could happen if she binds to Michael?"

"Worst case? Start of another Great War."

"Why would she want that though?"

Quinn shrugged. "I don't know, she's angry about something, but she's never told me what. Maybe this is her way of dealing with whatever it is. She wants the power, probably to get some kind of revenge on the Council; that's just what I think though. I just don't want to see her hurt; she's still my sister."

"And you don't have a brother called Jack, do you?"

"Huh?"

Mary smiled and leaned forward. "You don't even remember saying that, do you? When you first came to Tiani, you said you were looking for your brother."

"I had forgotten; it's just Cecilia and me. I don't want to lose her."

"I can understand that." Mary stood up and pulled on Quinn's hand to make him stand as well. "Let's find somewhere to put the bag down and then see what else this place has."

"Why not?"

The moved in and out of rooms until they found one that still had a roof covering it. Vines weaved up the walls and had created a curtain over the window. Dirt covered all the surfaces as Mary glanced around trying to decide which corner would serve best.

"We should set up in that corner," Mary said, and Quinn placed the supply bag down. "Should we try and...make it look better?"

"I don't think we need to, it's not completely horrid," Quinn replied.

Mary laughed and together they headed back into the main room and towards a flight of wide stairs. She tried to imagine how grand it must have looked once upon a time. The stones fit together without the mortar that most buildings had, and she wondered if magic had built it rather than hard work.

"Who do you think it belonged to?"

"No idea."

"Don't they teach you that? I mean, do you train to be a sorcerer?"

"They teach us to control our magic, we don't get history lessons. Everything we need to know is…It's a spell that has the knowledge we need to know."

"And nothing else? You never had extra questions? Never asked why?"

"I think most of us did, but you didn't ask why. We have an academy, like your school. The Sorcery Council oversees everything; in fact, they govern more than just that."

They had reached the top of the stairs and walked along the side of the floor they stood on, holding onto the vines that clung onto the small wall.

"Wow, you can see all the way to Riejan. The trees probably weren't so tall then when it was built." Mary leaned forward feeling confident that the stonework would hold. "I think that's the gathering rooms over there, up on the hill."

When Quinn didn't answer she turned her attention back on him. His fingers held onto a dark leather cord. Her eyes were drawn to the moulded filigree silver holder that hung from the cord with a little stone partially set inside it.

"Is that the stone…?"

Quinn nodded. "I felt bad, annoyed, maybe even a little angry, when I saw you'd left it behind. I wasn't quite sure what you meant by leaving it behind."

Mary stepped closer and reached out to tap the stone, sending it spinning before it settled back to its position.

"I left it behind because I knew I would use it again. I knew that if I took it…Cashel made it sound like you had no choice but to do what you were doing and that I was in the way. That there was something else out there waiting for you, and I didn't want to stand in your way of that."

"Here I thought you left it because you didn't want to see me again."

"Oh no, Quinn, it wasn't that at all." Mary placed her hand on his arm and he finally turned to look at her.

"Do you still want it? I mean…it isn't much now…the magic is all gone…but…well…I'd like you to still have it…it is yours after all." Quinn's voice was barely above a whisper as the setting sun lit the sky.

The light reflected from his eyes and she saw the blue-green eyes she wanted to become lost in.

"Yes, I would."

Quinn smiled and Mary pulled her braid to the side and turned to make it easier for him to place it around her neck. She felt the coolness of the stone as it settled against her skin. When she turned back, Quinn reached out for her and pulled her close. His arms circled her waist and she rested her head against his chest, closing her eyes as she listened to his heart beating.

Her hand reached up and found a similar cord to her own covered by the shirt he wore. Tugging gently at the cord, she pulled it from its concealment. A similar stone hung from a setting the same as her own. It felt warm in her hand as she held it.

"I never knew you had one too." Mary looked up at Quinn and saw him smiling down at her.

"It's how they work, the same type of stone infused with the magic of a sorcerer. The stones call to each other."

"That's really quite clever."

"Yeah."

"You could come back with me, Quinn, back to Tiani."

"I don't think I'll be much use in a school, but I can learn."

Reaching up, Mary rested her hand on the side of his face. Quinn rested his own hand on hers, and she felt his hand press against her waist. Her eyes focused on his face as flashes of the moment in his house filled her with anticipation. She knew only two things at that moment: that she would have her school and she would have the man she wanted there too.

"I'm sorry for all the trouble. Sorry for…"

"Shhh." She kissed him lightly on the lips. "You forget that I started it all in motion, maybe the book knew all along. Perhaps everything is going to be just as it was supposed to be."

"You believe this is all predestined?"

"Maybe a little of it is, but I think it's up to us to get there."

Quinn caressed the side of Mary's face and she felt the warmth of his lips as they found hers. She held his face in her hands as she kissed him back with just as much enthusiasm.

"We should head down the stairs before we can't see where we're going," Mary whispered.

"If I had my magic, I could have lit the way."

"Well this is more adventurous."

Quinn's laughter joined hers as they parted. Mary's hand grabbed his as they walked back down the stairs to the room where they'd left the supply pack. With each step, Mary enjoyed the happiness she felt and relished how alive she felt.

Once back in the room, Mary saw Quinn reach into his pocket and pull out the pouch.

"What's that?"

"From Cashel apparently." His fingers toyed with the string but didn't move to open it.

"Don't you want to know what's in it?"

"Yes and no."

"Come on, open it up."

Mary watched from beside Quinn as he tugged on the string and the pouch opened. She leaned in closer as Quinn reached in and pulled out a folded piece of paper.

"Is that all?" Mary asked disappointed.

"What were you expecting?"

"He's a sorcerer, right? Maybe some sparks of magic?"

Quinn laughed and kissed her on the forehead. "Not sure the magic ever worked the way you think it does. Well, let's see what the paper is."

With the paper unfolded, Quinn held it up to try and catch the last of the light before it disappeared.

"What does it say?" Mary asked

"I don't know, I can't read it anymore. I guess without the magic I lose everything it gave me. Here."

Mary took the piece of paper and squinted at it to try and make out the writing. It says, "Power does not possess people; people possess power."

Mary heard the quiet sigh they left Quinn's lips. "You were hoping for more?"

"If I had my magic...maybe I could have stopped Cecilia."

"Are you sure you want to try and stop her..."

"I must Mary...I may not be a sorcerer any longer, but I still made the pledge at the Academy...I must try at least. Besides, Cecilia would never hurt me; she'd argue, but never do anything else."

CHAPTER TWENTY-EIGHT

Quinn and Mary dismounted the horse and hurried up the steps and into the Gathering Room. They paused inside the room partially concealed by the drape that separated the entrance from the main room. Mary peered through the gap and saw Prater standing up front near the preparation rooms.

"Sorceress," his voice echoed around the empty room.

Mary stepped to the side to allow Quinn a view of the scene as well. As they watched, one of the doors opened and Cecilia appeared with her arms folded across her chest.

"This is neither the time nor the place, Prater," she hissed and turned towards the door.

"We had a deal sorceress and you failed to keep your end of the agreement!"

Prater took a step towards Cecilia, and she spun around with her hand outstretched.

"You're not going to try anything foolish, surely, Prater. I really thought that you were smarter than that."

"You made a deal with me."

Cecilia groaned and raised her hand towards the door beside her own.

"What's she doing?" Mary whispered to Quinn as the edge of the door shone blue before returning to normal.

"She's sealing Michael in the room; probably for the best that he doesn't see any of this."

"Let's get one thing straight, Prater, yes, we made a deal, but you left out an important detail." Cecilia pointed her finger towards him. "You never stated a timeframe."

"Neither did you, sorceress."

"What do you think he's going to do?" Mary whispered to Quinn who shrugged in response.

Prater took another step towards Cecilia until he stood an arm's length away from her.

"Don't think that you can get away without holding up your end of the bargain," Prater stated.

"Could we possibly settle this *after* the ceremony? It just seems a little...inappropriate to deal with this at the moment," Cecilia replied with a smile.

"We'll deal with it now." Prater seemed determined on the matter.

"What type of bargain do you think they made?" Quinn asked as he turned to Mary.

"She came to see Prater, while I was staying there. They made a deal that if he could find a spell that would break the binding then she would give him something in return."

"Why didn't you say something?"

Mary shrugged. "It just didn't seem possible that he would find such a spell. I've spent far more time in the book building than he ever did, and I never found anything like that."

"Stay here, Mary."

Mary reached out and held his upper arm. "Quinn..."

"Please, Mary, stay here."

She heard the pleading in his voice, but didn't want him going out there, not with both Cecilia and Prater to face. His hands reached out and held her face. She sighed as her mind tried to process the possible outcomes for all.

"Mary, you've got your plans for the future – you need to be safe so that can happen."

Mary nodded, but said no more to Quinn as he released his hold. He crouched down before he crept out from behind the drape he kept low to the ground concealed by the seats as he moved down the aisle.

"Perhaps it is you, Prater, who doesn't get the gravity of the situation – we'll deal with it *later*," Cecilia hissed.

"Sorceress, I know the rules and my rights in our deal. You need to follow through, now." Prater took a step back as Cecilia growled and moved towards him. "Just like a sorceress, you really thought you could outsmart a human, didn't you? I broke that binding and I will have my reward."

Cecilia smiled at him as she took another step forward. She pointed her finger out towards him and he took several steps backwards in response. Behind the drape, Mary shifted her feet; she felt uncomfortable hiding away doing nothing constructive.

A door opening on the other side of the platform drew everyone's attention across the room. A short little man holding a book looked up to see Prater and Cecilia. In the aisle, Quinn crouched down to stay out of sight.

"Binding man…" Cecilia's voice wavered, and she lowered her hand.

"I see you are both ready for me, but where are the witnesses? I need two for the ceremony to go ahead."

"Oh please, give me some credit, binding man. You honestly think this is the man I want to be bound too?"

"Hey, what's that supposed to mean?" Prater objected.

"Oh dear, I'm not from here…" he picked up a sheet of paper that had been resting on the top of the book. "Cecilia, is it? Forgive me, child."

"Forgiven, binding man, but you're not needed here yet." She smiled at the little man and tilted her head to the side, and her red hair fell to cover her shoulder.

"I'm not sure what to make of this, young lady, perhaps we should withdraw to the room on the side and confer for a moment…"

"We don't have to do that. Cecilia, I think it is quite clear that I broke the binding between Michael and Mary; how long could it possibly take for you to just grant my end of the bargain and be rid of me?" Prater said.

At the back of the Gathering Room, Mary whispered to herself: "What does he mean he broke the binding? Quinn broke the binding…he said he had seen the dragons…he lost his power because…" Mary watched on as Cecilia and Prater stared each other down. The binding man shuffled his feet. Quinn, still crouched down, moved down the aisle keeping close to the seats.

Quinn reached the first row of the seats and paused. Mary watched as he turned and looked back in her direction, sparing a smile for her. Her hands gripped the drape as Quinn stood up and walked towards the trio.

"Break the spell, sister," Quinn's voice broke the silence and drew the attention of all three towards him.

Prater turned sharply to face Quinn while Cecilia leaned to the side to look at him as he came into view.

"Well hello, baby brother, fancy you coming to my binding, too. Today really is my day for being popular for once."

"Come on, Cecilia, you're getting what you want."

"You want me to take my little spell off that girl?"

Quinn nodded, "I broke the binding; now remove the spell."

"How do I know it was *you* who broke the binding? That man in front of you says *he* broke the binding, and for all I know he might actually be telling the truth – as unbelievable as that is seeing that he is a mortal."

"Sister, please remove what remains of the spell on Mary. Let this all end here - walk away now before the Sorcery Council act. Sister, the Three Kingdoms can't go to war again..." Quinn took a step towards her with his hand outstretched. "...please."

Cecilia tapped her foot on the ground, and it echoed around the room. Her gaze skipped between the two men and as she placed her hands on her hips

"What, before I am bound to Michael?"

"Young lady, it would seem..." the binding man began as he watched Cecilia.

"Urgh, I don't have time to listen to you!" Cecilia raised her hand and the binding man froze with his mouth open. "Look, and this goes for both of you, let the ceremony be done with first. After that, I promise that both of you shall have what you want. I can't be more generous than that, now can I?"

"I don't trust you, sorceress."

"My sister is a lot of things, Prater, but she does keep her word."

"Don't think I have finished with you. I don't know how you passed that test, but Quinn, you betrayed me, and I don't forgive easily."

Quinn increased the distance between himself and Prater; Mary noticed though that he didn't move any closer to his sister as he did so.

"What's that meant to mean?" Cecilia's hand glowed. "That almost sounded like you were threatening my brother."

Prater smiled at her magic that swirled in a ball just above her hand. "You can't use that against me. I know the rules, too. Books can be so informative!"

Mary felt a gush of air behind her and she turned to look out of the open doors. A red dragon landed on the steps and her heart skipped. Frozen, she saw the dragon bobbing his head to the side, and Mary frowned at it. This is what she had read about, thought about, wanted to receive some good luck from. Her breathing quickened as she stared up at it waiting to see what it would do with her.

"Open the drapes a bit, girl, come on. I don't have all day."

"Bad luck?"

The dragon flicked his tail. "Luck? Good luck, bad luck, girl. I've heard about you, have you learnt nothing? Make your own luck; we dragons have better things to do."

Mary opened her mouth to reply but decided against saying anything. Reaching behind her, she fumbled around for the cord while her eyes continued to be trained on the dragon. When her fingers brushed against the heavy fabric again, she relented and turned away from the dragon. Her eyes found the cord and she pulled on it, opening the drapes fully.

The dragon took a few steps forward into the building, before settling himself down to the side where Mary had concealed herself. He stared directly towards the front of the small entrance room. Mary stood awkwardly beside the cord, concealed from the room for a while longer but nervous at the dragon being so close.

"Hey, I can't open the door. Can someone try opening the door please?" Michael's muffled voice called out from his temporary prison.

"I'll see if I can find someone, Michael," Cecilia called back loudly

"Break it now, sister!" Quinn's voice reiterated.

"How many times do I need to say it! Once I am bound, and not a moment before." Cecilia's set face glowered at her brother.

"Cecilia." Prater waved a piece of paper in her direction. She eyed it for a moment before snarling in frustration.

Cecilia's face changed to a glowering look of anger as she flung magic she held behind her, hitting Michael's door. She flung out her arm sharply towards Quinn, sending a wave of magic forward. Quinn sailed above the rows of seats then collided hard with the stone wall at the back of the room, crumpling into a heap at the base of it.

A gasp escaped Mary's lips and she covered her mouth. She looked over at the dragon who watched her for a moment before looking forward again. Leaning forward, she held the drape as she looked around it to see Quinn leaning against the wall, still not moving.

Mary glanced back towards the front to see Michael leaving the room he'd been in. When he glanced up, he paused seeing Prater before him.

"You? What are you doing here?" Michael demanded and stepped up beside a startled Cecilia.

"Ah, I remember you, too. You really have no idea who it is you are going to be bound to, do you?"

"What are you talking about?" Michael's gaze alternated between Cecilia and Prater, eventually it settled on Cecilia. "Cecilia, what's going on here? Why are these people here? And why is the binding man looking like that?"

"I'll give you a moment to explain." Prater stepped back and waved the paper before tucking it inside his shirt. He strode to the back of the room.

The dragon puffed out some smoke, and the drape fell back into place, tangling Mary in it. She stepped back and glared at the dragon. Moving towards the opening, she watched as Michael grabbed hold of Cecilia's arms and turned her to face him. Mary couldn't hear what Michael said as his words were drowned out by Prater's boots that had already passed the drapes.

Mary opened the drapes enough to look towards Quinn. Her grip loosened on the drapes as she saw his eyes flicker open. She sighed in relief. Prater had reached Quinn and crouched in front of him.

"You betrayed me."

"You don't understand..." No further words were spoken.

He looked down at the knife protruding from his stomach which Prater skilfully retracted, wiping the blood on Quinn's sleeve.

CHAPTER
TWENTY-NINE

"No!" Mary clamped her hands over her mouth as all eyes fell on her.

Quinn shook his head as he held his hands over the wound and tried to slow down the blood that escaped through his fingers.

Prater sneered at Mary before standing up and whispering. "Nobody betrays me."

Up at the front Cecilia waved her hand towards the binding man. He stumbled forward and his forehead creased at the scene before him. Cecilia turned to him and threatened, "Bind us quickly or your life will not be worth living."

"Sorceress!" Prater turned to face Cecilia again, obstructing her view of Quinn.

"What now? This should not be so complicated!"

"Sorceress, you owe me," Prater demanded, "and I warned you not to dismiss me so lightly!"

"I don't want to deal with this at the moment!"

She raised her hand to dismiss Prater, but he moved forward purposefully allowing Quinn's body to come into her view.

"That's not possible, I only pushed him back...what did you do to my brother?"

Mary couldn't wait any longer. Moving out from the drapes she rushed to Quinn's side, picking up his hand in her left she tried to stir him into opening his eyes again. Putting her own hands over the wound she pressed down hard.

"Too late, Mary," Prater said, and she turned to see him walk back towards Cecilia.

With tears in her eyes she turned back to Quinn. She could see his chest rising and falling but it seemed shallow. She pressed down harder on the wound, but the blood continued to escape.

"Quinn, Quinn, look at me."

"Sorceress, I won't ask you again to make good on the deal we made."

"Prater, what did you do to my brother?"

"Complete the agreement and perhaps you can save him," Prater stated.

"I can't undo what you have done!" Cecilia's eyes narrowed on Prater; without turning around she ordered, "Binding man: leave."

"But you said...I haven't..."

The binding man saw Prater raise the knife in his direction. He gulped and turned to see the unmoving man at the back of the room. When Prater stepped closer again, the binding man turned and headed towards the room he had emerged from.

"Cecilia you should have told me. How could you keep something that important from me?" Michael let go of her and stepped away, careful not to get any closer to Prater. "What have you done?"

"You stupid fool! We could have had more power than you could ever dream of!" Cecilia waved her hand at Michael and he shifted backwards into the room once again. The door slammed shut and glowed.

"Just leaves us to settle things then." Prater sheathed the knife into his boot. "You will pay, sorceress."

"I will not, you fool – why did you harm my brother?" Cecilia sneered and raised her hand.

"He betrayed me – must run in the family. The Academy has rules about not keeping your end of a bargain. Hope you remember what the consequence is for breaking a deal with a mortal."

With the blood not stopping, Mary turned back towards the drapes. *Perhaps the dragon can help with this.* Before she could move, the drapes shifted to the sides. One side caught on a nail above the doorway and Mary closed her eyes in disappointment – the dragon no longer sat crouched to the side. The space was empty.

Mary heard Prater chanting and when she looked his way she saw him reading from the paper he'd produced earlier. Prater continued and the noise stirred Quinn, his eyes opening slightly.

"What's that? That's not like the chants or spells that we learnt," Quinn whispered.

"Shh. We need to worry about you at the moment."

Quinn stared past Mary and she turned to see Cecilia looking pale as Prater continued to chant.

"No, wait, Prater," Cecilia called out and lowered her hand.

Prater didn't stop reading, and Cecilia closed her eyes. Mustering the magic she possessed, she sent a spray of blue light towards Prater as he finished speaking, before she collapsed to the ground in a heap.

The room seemed motionless for several heartbeats. Cecilia lay on the ground, though not dead because her body rose and fell as she breathed. Where Prater once stood, the cries of a baby rang out.

A door opened and the binding man emerged once again. He looked around the room before running towards the entrance. Rounding the drapes, he skidded to a stop as a dragon padded inside.

"Don't eat me!" The binder's plea drew Mary's attention and she smiled at seeing the dragon. She watched the dragon raise his eye ridge in response before nodding towards Mary.

"Bind them."

The binder looked confused. The dragon puffed grey smoke creating enough of a breeze for the binder's hair to become messy.

"Bind who?" the binder growled in frustration and rubbed his weary eyes.

"Bind them," the dragon repeated and looked into the Gathering Room. The binder followed the dragon's gaze to Quinn and Mary.

"Us?" Mary whispered as the dragon nudged the binder from behind making him move closer.

With Quinn's eyes closed again, Mary shook her head. "Please dragon, I just need help, a little good luck. Please…"

"I can't, I need both to give permission. I'm not about to break the rules in order to satisfy a whim." The binder stared back stubbornly at the dragon.

"Bind them…or I'll eat you." The dragon moved his eyes closer to the binder who gulped several times.

"Eat me?"

"Eat you…starting with your feet."

"Fine, but I'm doing this under protest!"

The dragon puffed smoke in reply and nodded. Settling down, his eyes followed the binding man as he approached Mary and Quinn.

"You have both agreed to be bound together in both love and commitment. What is bound let no one divide," the binder murmured.

"Quinn, you must open your eyes."

Mary looked down at her hands to see the blood running between her fingers and down to the skirt of her dress. She felt a strange but familiar sensation on her hand and watched as a binding mark faded in on her left hand; a corresponding one on Quinn's.

The binder nodded at the dragon as he walked back towards him. "That man needs help and you've delayed me to bind them? If he dies it will be on your conscious." He skirted around the dragon and out the entrance door. The dragon remained.

Mary bit her lip and held Quinn's hand tightly. "Quinn, please. It's not your time to go. It can't be your time to go."

"Mary, you'll have the best school," Quinn whispered hoarsely. His eyes opened as he reached up and pulled Mary closer to him, lightly kissing her on her lips. "Don't ever forget me. I love you..."

"No, you can't die." Quinn's eyelids closed once again. Mary turned in desperation, "Cecilia, please – please Cecilia."

Using her hands, Cecilia pushed herself up from the floor. She turned, looked across the room to Mary and her brother, and glanced away; her hair in disarray, her dress torn and stained, and her magic gone.

"There's nothing I can do." Cecilia shook her head. The cries of the nearby baby captured her attention. He sat on the floor surrounded by familiar black clothing. Wrapping the baby in the shirt, she picked him up and begun walking towards her brother.

"But you're a sorceress!"

"I *was* a sorceress."

"Quinn." Mary relaxed the pressure on the wound as tears welled in her eyes. Desperately she grabbed Quinn's hand tightly in hers. His other hand slipped in the blood and fell to the floor. Closing her eyes tightly she asked for one piece of good luck. "It was sixteen, lucky sixteen. Quinn, I want you there with me whether that's Tiani, or somewhere else. Please don't leave me."

A cough. Mary's eyes flew open as a blue glow dissipated from around Quinn. When she looked, she saw no trace of the wound except for the blood stains.

"How?" Cecilia sat on the other side of her brother. Her hand reached out and pulled back on the cut fabric of his shirt, his skin flawless of marks despite the blood stains. Quinn's eyes slowly opened.

"Huh, guess Prater was right after all, he did break the binding otherwise you would be magicless," Cecilia half-smiled at her comment, but added: "You're bloody lucky, little brother, you know that, don't you?"

"Our transaction is over, sorcerer," the sound of the dragon's voice drew the attention of all in the group.

"Jharobi, I don't understand. Why do I have my magic back?"

"You never relinquished your magic, sorcerer," Jharobi paused and inclined his head to the side as he watched Quinn. "Prater broke the binding, only a moment or two before you agreed to release your powers."

"But...why didn't you tell me that?" Quinn stammered and unsuccessfully attempted to push himself up. "Why wasn't I affected by the gold in Tiani?"

Jharobi mustered a smile, "Sorcerer, you no longer had the heart of a sorcerer. You may as well have had no magic at all; if you'd read the book on the subject you would know that a sorcerer's magic is linked with his desire to *perform* it. You had made up your mind, and I simply played along."

"People possess power," Mary muttered, remembering the words on the paper.

"That's right, you accessed his power. Just like the humans once did a long time ago."

"What's with the baby then?" Quinn watched as his sister held the now quiet infant in her arms.

"I kept my end of the bargain with Prater," Cecilia replied with a shrug of her shoulders and smiled.

Quinn laughed at the expression on his sister's face, "So, he wanted to be younger, then?"

"I made him what he wanted."

"So that's Prater?" Mary questioned unsure if she had understood. Cecilia confirmed it with a smile.

"But what about the Golden Law, Jharobi? What you did breaks the treaty, doesn't it?" Quinn asked.

"Not to mention makes dragons a bit hypocritical since, you know, given what just happened," Cecilia added, watching Jharobi.

"Another technicality – *I* asked for you to be bound, you both had little choice in the matter...plus, technically you were almost mortal when you were bound. Quinn we dragons saw that you were willing to lose everything in order to prevent history being repeated, that carried a lot of weight with us. The Dragon Council decided to consult with the Sorcery Council on this matter...for a change we actually agreed," Jharobi smiled and spread his wings. "That's my work done; keep to your promise, Quinn. You have born a great deal in your short life, but nothing will weigh more than the responsibility you and Mary now have to humans, sorcerers, and dragons; don't ever abuse that trust we have in you or exploit the power you have."

"That's all well and good, but where does that leave me? I did keep my end of the bargain!" Cecilia shouted but Jharobi didn't turn back once as he left the room.

Quinn and Mary both smiled. "Now what?"

The thundering of boots on the steps drew their attention to the door. Delwyn and six men from Tiani stood ready with weapons drawn.

"Where's Master Prater?" he demanded.

Cecilia pushed herself up from the floor before picking up the crying baby.

"That's Prater's shirt." Delwyn looked again at the baby; at length, he leaned forward. His eyes glanced at Cecilia who smiled before she held the baby out to him. He awkwardly took the baby.

"That's his shirt alright," Cecila replied.

"What's it doing on the baby?"

"Well, it's like this...earlier today, that wasn't a baby. In fact, this morning that was a rather arrogant man who needed to learn to treat people better; a lesson it seems I also have to learn."

"Wait, so what you're saying...No, that can't be. Are you saying that this isn't just Prater's shirt? This...baby...it's Prater?"

"Yes, and he is all yours now." Cecilia turned and started walking back towards Mary and Quinn.

"Mine? What am I meant to do with a baby? What am I going to tell everyone back in Tiani?" Delwyn turned to his men who backed off slightly. "Great, you know, my mother always told me to never mess with anything I didn't understand completely. I guess she'll be pleased when I tell her she's correct. Ah Master, this is why humans are not meant to mess with magic."

"We could leave him here," one of the men suggested.

"We'll find someone to help here in the city before we head back to Tiani. I don't want to be the one responsible for making that decision. Imagine having to grow up a second time. Do you think he'll remember the first time?"

Delwyn and his men continued their conversation as they walked out of the Gathering Room. The atmosphere in the room now lighter than it had been.

Cecilia held out her hand to Quinn; he took it and she helped pull him up to his feet. "Steady now.

I guess I should be pleased that you finally took my advice, baby brother."

"How so?"

"You finally got a life."

Quinn smiled as Mary stood up beside him and took his hand in hers and squeezed it.

"Don't get used to it sister, this was a one-off occasion"

"How does it feel?"

"Feel, how do you think I feel Cecilia? I feel like someone slammed me into a wall."

"You'll get over it, but that's not what I meant. You were human for a while there."

Mary turned to look at Quinn as he nodded and smiled. "You won't hate me if I say that I'm really happy to have my magic back, will you?"

"No, I think I can overlook that."

Quinn turned back to his sister as they sneared the front entrance. "What will you do now?"

Cecilia brushed down her dress. "I'm not really sure, Quinn. The last thing I expected today was to walk away as a human - I was supposed to be some all-powerful sorceress. How you managed to get what I wanted...Well, that's still hypocritical in my books."

Mary smiled back at her new sister. "I'm sure you'll do fine as a human."

Cecilia half-smiled. "You know, Mary, you had already broken the spell I cast over you. I'm guessing you found some determination and stopped waiting for someone else to fix everything."

"But I can't read as well as I used to."

"You will, it will take time to come back, but it will." Cecilia reached out and hugged Quinn. He reached out his free hand and returned the gesture. "I love you, Quinn, even if you have managed to destroy my plans."

"You're not as angry as I thought you'd be."

"What would the point be? I'll probably find a pillow to hurt later on in private, but I knew the consequences I might have to face."

"Then why do all this?"

Cecilia looked away to the floor for a moment before she sighed. "There are some things I never told you. Things that the The Academy did. Things to do with our parents."

"Our parents?"

"Not today, brother, today you need to rest, and I need to go and vent, maybe try this human thing of drowning my sorrows. Tomorrow I'll think about facing everything else."

"Will you be okay?"

Cecilia hugged Quinn before she pulled away. "You know me Quinn; I always land on my feet, even when the ground below them is gone. I know that there's one thing about me that will never change."

"What's that?" Quinn asked.

"No matter what happens in my life now, I will still live it to the full with no regrets."

"As shall I."

"As shall we, Quinn, together," Mary said and leaned her head on his shoulder, dreaming of the possibilities her future now held. "We will make our own future and our own luck."

Jenni lives in Australia and
loves all things magical.

Reviews of her work are
welcome on any platform.

You can find information
about all her books
on her website

www.jenniwardauthor.com.au